Has Anyone Seen Jessica Jenkins?

Has Anyone Seen Jessica Jenkins?

LIZ KESSLER

CANDLEWICK PRESS

Copyright © 2014 by Liz Kessler

First published in Great Britain by Orion Children's Books, a division of the Orion Publishing Group

First U.S. edition 2015

Library of Congress Catalog Card Number 2014944676
ISBN 978-0-7636-7060-3

15 16 17 18 19 20 BVG 10 9 8 7 6 5 4 3 2 1

Printed in Berryville, VA, U.S.A.

This book was typeset in Sabon.

Candlewick Press
99 Dover Street
Somerville, Massachusetts 02144

visit us at www.candlewick.com

ACKNOWLEDGMENTS

As always, this book could not have been written without the help and support of some very special people. So I would like to say a special thank-you to the usual suspects—you know who you are. (And in case you don't, you are mostly Laura, Mom, and Dad. Oh, and not-so-usual suspect John Dougherty, for the fab title!)

I would like to give a big thank-you to my publishers, Orion and Candlewick, and my agent, Catherine Clarke, who all went above and beyond what anyone would expect in terms of support and patience as I battled to get this book written. You all knew that I would get there in the end, even if I wasn't so sure! I hope that you'll all think the final result was worth it.

But the biggest thank-you of all is reserved for Amber Caravéo. Amber, you sweated over this book almost as much as I did—and to show my gratitude for your extreme commitment, hard work, and loyalty to your authors and their books, this one is dedicated to you.

Chapter 1

It was during a Friday afternoon double geography class that I first discovered I had superhuman powers.

I bet you think that sounds exciting. Well, if it's never happened to you, then take it from me: it isn't. It's scary. And weird. And, if it involves not knowing the answer when the teacher asks you to explain the effects of coastal erosion on prehistoric rock formations, it can also get you into a lot of trouble.

But I'm getting ahead of myself. So let's start from the beginning. Well, not the *actual* beginning. That'll come later. But let's at least get back to geography class.

It was mid-April and an unseasonably warm day. I'd spent the lunch break swapping gossip, weekend plans, and chocolate cookies with my best friend, Izzy Williams, and was settling down to geography when three things converged to make me tired.

Thing one: the chocolate cookies. Chocolate *always* makes me sleepy.

Thing two: the sun had crept out from behind a bunch of clouds and was beaming like a spotlight through the window and straight onto my desk.

Thing three: Ms. Cooper announced that today's lesson would be about coastal erosion and prehistoric rock formations.

I think you'll agree that the odds were stacked against me.

I could hear Ms. Cooper's voice in the distant background of my mind, saying something about cliffs and rocks and tidal patterns. A minute later, I was halfway into a dream in which I was lying on a sandy beach at the bottom of the cliffs. A savage prod in my ribs jolted me off the beach and back into the classroom.

I glared at Izzy. "What was that for?" I hissed.

She didn't reply. Instead she nodded toward the front of the class. Ms. Cooper was staring at me, her mouth pursed in a frown, the word "Well?" dripping from her lips. I wiped away a tiny bit of drool that was dripping from mine and glanced helplessly around the room.

A few sympathetic faces were turned toward me. The others were mostly looking away. They knew what it was like.

"I—I'm sorry, Ms. Cooper. I didn't quite understand. Could you please repeat the question?" I tried.

Ms. Cooper pursed her lips even tighter so that her mouth practically disappeared. "See me after class," she said, then snapped her head away from me and pointed at Heather Berry in the front row. "Heather, perhaps you can answer?"

Typical.

Let me tell you about Heather Berry. She's kind of the opposite of me.

Me: small and nondescript. Long brown hair, which never seems to do much except hang there, and greenish-gray eyes that you have to stare hard at to even notice.

Heather: tallest girl in the class, ridiculously skinny, amazingly shiny blond hair, and eyes that are so perfectly blue I have occasionally wondered if she wears those specially colored contact lenses.

Me: usually seen in scruffy jeans and random tops, like combat jackets or baggy sweaters discovered while browsing around thrift shops on a Saturday afternoon.

Heather: always sports the latest designer clothes—so trendy she's often seen wearing the "in" thing before it's even in.

Me: shortish attention span and tendency to pass notes with Izzy rather than *always* listen to the teacher—hence my tendency to get scolded a lot. Except in English, which I love. The English teacher, Mr. Martins, is cool. He has the longest handlebar mustache in the world, a completely bald head, and a million earrings in each ear. Plus, he occasionally makes his classes interesting and seems to think I'm not stupid.

Heather: probably every teacher's favorite student. Always listens, always volunteers to help. Captain of the volleyball team and class president. Always surrounded by about five girls who hang on her every word and copy her every move, as well as at least five boys who want to be her boyfriend. Looks down her nose at anyone who isn't part of her group of friends/worshippers.

You might have gathered that Heather is not my favorite person in the world.

She glanced around at me, glaring as if I were a piece of dirt that had accidentally gotten stuck on her shoe, then turned back to the teacher.

As Heather calmly explained the finer details of coastal erosion on a local prehistoric site, I breathed out and tried to think up some strategies for staying awake till the end of class.

I tore a piece of paper from my notebook, scribbled *What did I miss?* on it, and passed it to Izzy under the table.

Izzy opened the note and read it. She started to write something on it. Then she scribbled it out, scrunched the paper into a ball, and chewed on the end of her pen.

Uh-oh.

See, Izzy and I go back as far as I can remember. I know her about as well as I know myself. Better, sometimes. And I know that when she chews the end of her pen, it means she's worried about something. The only thing that indicates even more trouble than chewing the end of her pen is if she takes her glasses off and nibbles the end of them. Izzy has about fifty pairs of glasses and changes them whenever she changes her outfit. Today was a school day, so she was wearing her blue ones, to match our uniform.

I tore another piece of paper from my book. *What's up?* I wrote.

Izzy read the note. Then she took off her glasses and nibbled on the end of them.

Double uh-oh.

Finally, she put her glasses back on, scribbled something on the piece of paper, and passed the note back.

Can't explain now. Tell you on the way home.

And I don't know why, but something about her words made me feel even more nervous than the thought of my appointment with Ms. Cooper.

Izzy was waiting for me in the coatroom.

"What did she say?" she asked as she passed me my coat and we made our way across the school yard.

"Just the standard 'You need to take your work more seriously' lecture," I said, pulling on my coat and slinging my bag over my shoulder.

"Could be worse," Izzy said.

"Yeah." Ms. Cooper had been known to keep students behind for an hour, copying out articles from *National Geographic* and rearranging the objects on her nature table, so I'd gotten off easy.

"So what's the thing you couldn't tell me earlier?" I asked. Izzy hadn't met my eyes since we'd come out of the school building.

She glanced furtively around, as if we were being watched. Nudging her head toward the park, she pulled me across the road. "In here," she said.

We often went home through Smeaton's Park. In the summer, there was usually an ice-cream truck outside the gates, and there was a lake in the middle of the park where we'd throw the crusts from our lunch boxes to the ducks that gathered there.

We sat down on a bench at the edge of the lake.

"Iz, what's going on?" I asked. "You're worrying me."

"*I'm* worrying *you?*" she said with a laugh. And not a *ha-ha-you're-so-funny* laugh. More of an *I'm-sitting-with-a-crazy-person-and-I-need-to-escape-without-letting-them-know-I'm-scared* laugh.

"Izzy," I said firmly, "I'm your best friend. If there's something wrong, you can tell me."

She turned away and nodded. Eventually, she looked back at me. "Something weird happened, back there, in geography class," she said finally.

"You mean my falling asleep and getting into trouble? That's not weird. It happens all the—"

"Not that," she said. She pointed at my arm. "Your elbow."

"My *elbow*?" I repeated, lifting my arm to look at it. "What's wrong with my elbow?"

"Nothing now," Izzy said. "But back then, it . . . it . . ."

"It what?"

Izzy took another breath. "It disappeared," she said.

"My elbow disappeared," I echoed.

Izzy nodded. "And it wasn't just your elbow. It started there, but it was beginning to spread along your arm." She paused and leaned toward me. "Something weird was happening."

Something weird was *definitely* happening. My best friend was going crazy. "*What* was happening?" I asked.

"I think . . ." She leaned closer and glanced over her shoulder to check that we were alone. Then she lowered her voice and spoke again, and this time, her words made me shudder: "I think you were turning invisible."

Chapter 2

Which is not what you expect your best friend to say to you, sitting in the park at 4:05 on a Friday afternoon. Or at any other time on any other day, in fact.

I stared at Izzy and tried to find some words that might form themselves into a sentence that could possibly pass as an adequate reply. I finally came up with *"Whaaa?"*

Which didn't really pass the test of being either a sentence or an adequate reply, but it was all I had.

Izzy at least had the courtesy to blush. "Hey, don't shoot the messenger, OK? I'm just telling you what I saw."

"Or didn't see, more to the point," I replied.

Izzy laughed. I glared at her. She stopped laughing.

"Look, I'm probably wrong," she said. "I mean, it was most likely the light or something. You know, the sun shining in my eyes."

"Yeah, probably."

Izzy laughed again. This time I didn't glare at her. "I mean, imagine thinking you were turning invisible!" she said.

I laughed, too, beginning to relax. "I know. Crazy, huh?"

"What an idiot! In fact, now that I think about it, I'm *certain* it was the light. The sun was shining right on you. That's definitely what it was."

"Good. I'm glad we figured that out," I said, delving into my bag and pulling out my lunch box. "Now, are we going to feed the ducks or what?"

We threw our crusts into the lake and watched the ducks come flying over, then quack as they slid into their watery landings and pecked up the bread.

We laughed and pointed and gossiped and chatted the whole time. Like we normally do. When the bread was all gone, we made plans for meeting up the next day and texting each other the minute we got home. Like we normally do.

In fact, if you'd been watching us, you wouldn't have noticed anything different from usual.

You'd only have known anything was different if you were inside my mind.

See, Izzy had hit on something that I didn't want to say out loud. The thing was, I'd been having some odd feelings lately. Mainly when I was tired. I couldn't really put the feelings into words. If I tried to, I'd probably use words like *fuzzy* or *woozy* or *weird*.

I told you: not exactly much to go on. All I knew was that I hadn't been feeling a hundred percent my normal self lately. And Izzy's words had made me admit that.

Not out loud. I wasn't ready to do that yet. But to myself. And that was bad enough.

I went straight to my bedroom after dinner. I told Mom and Dad I wanted to get all my homework out of the way before the weekend, which was enough to keep them off my back.

What I really wanted to do was try to find a way to prove—or preferably *dis*prove—what Izzy had said. She'd said it had started when I was falling asleep, so I figured all I had to do was lie down and start nodding off, and see what happened.

I took off my shoes and drew the curtains.

Then I lay down on the bed and closed my eyes. My mind was spinning with questions. What if Izzy was right? What if something really weird *was* happening to me? What then?

I shook my head and forced myself not to focus on what Izzy had said. It was crazy. It was impossible.

I made myself yawn and tried to convince myself I was tired. After a few more minutes, I realized that, actually, I *was* quite tired. I could feel myself nodding off. This was it. I was going to find out. I just needed to . . .

Which was when it hit me. How on earth was I supposed to see what was happening to my body while I was falling asleep? The moment I opened my eyes to see what was going on, I wouldn't be falling asleep anymore!

There was only one way I could do this.

I went downstairs. Mom and Dad were on the love seat with the TV on.

"Can Izzy come for a sleepover?"

"I thought you wanted to get all your home-work done," Mom said.

"I've done most of it."

"That was quick," Dad said as he flicked through the channels with the remote.

"Izzy can help. We can do the rest together. Anyway, it's Friday. It's not like it's a school night."

Dad looked at Mom and shrugged. "I don't see why not," he said.

"As long as it's OK with her parents," Mom added.

I was already out the door and halfway through a text to Izzy. "Thank you!" I yelled behind me.

So, I don't know if you've ever tried it, but it turns out that trying to go to sleep, at least three hours before bedtime, while someone is staring at you, is not actually all that easy.

"Close your eyes!" Izzy yelled for the seventeenth time.

"I can't sleep while you're looking at me!"

"But that's the whole point! How am I supposed to see what's happening if I'm not looking?"

I sighed and sat up. "This isn't going to work," I said. "I'm not even tired."

"Shall we go for a jog?" Izzy offered.

I gave her a look that I hoped communicated an adequate level of horror and disgust.

"I'm just trying to think of ways to make you tired."

"I've got an idea," I said. I powered up my laptop.

Izzy craned her neck to look over my shoulder while I typed. "What are you doing?"

"I'm looking for a boring video to watch," I explained.

"Ooh, good idea. Something about politics or the weather or history." Then she pointed at the screen. "How about that one?" She was pointing at a program called *Money Wars,* described as "an in-depth look at Britain's economic strategy in the 1930s."

"That ought to do it," I agreed, and clicked on the button to start the program.

It worked like a charm. Within five minutes, my eyes began to close.

Almost immediately, I heard my name being called as something grabbed my arm and shook me. I opened my eyes with a start. Sitting up, I stared at Izzy. She was still holding on to my arm, her fingernails digging into my sweater.

I stretched and yawned. Izzy let go of my sleeve.

"So?" I asked. "Anything happen? Why were you shaking my arm?"

"To wake you up," she said, not looking at me. Before I had the chance to tell her I hadn't actually fallen asleep in the space of the twenty seconds I'd had my eyes closed, she added, "But it took me a few tries to find it."

"I'm guessing you eventually tracked it down, hanging from my shoulder as usual?" I replied in as light a tone as I could manage.

Izzy finally looked at me. "Your arm was completely invisible," she said.

I stared at Izzy. "My arm . . ." I said limply.

"Was invisible, yes. Both of them, in fact. And your feet."

"My feet," I repeated, nodding slowly.

"Your head was starting to go, too," Izzy went on. "That was when I yelled your name. It was getting freaky."

"It was *getting* freaky?"

"Well, it was getting beyond freaky," Izzy admitted.

We sat without speaking for . . . how long? Five minutes? An hour? Neither of us knew what to say. Unsurprisingly. Would you?

So instead, we took turns opening our mouths, realizing we still didn't have any words to describe or explain what was happening, then closing them again.

"We need a strategy," I said eventually.

Izzy smiled. I was finally talking her language. Izzy *loves* strategies. For her, they're the next best thing to new notebooks or chess clubs.

See, Izzy and I are kind of soul sisters and kind of complete opposites at the same time. She isn't big on thrift shops, and I don't hyperventilate over shelves full of stationery, but we're happy to put up with both if it means spending a Saturday afternoon in town together. Equally, I do not get what's exciting about moving knights (which don't look anything like knights), kings (which don't look anything like kings), and bishops (etc.) around a checkered board. Izzy likes nothing more. Good thing we have Tom in our lives for that.

Tom Johnson is a boy I grew up with. Our moms were in the same maternity ward, and Tom and I were born on the same day. Tom's grandparents live in Jamaica and his dad was away visiting them, since Tom wasn't due for another three weeks, so his mom was on her own and she and my mom got to know each other. Our moms have remained good friends ever since.

I think they had this idea that Tom and I would get married one day if they took us to playgroup together often enough. Tom is cute. He has gorgeous brown skin, big brown eyes, and crazy black, ringletty hair. He's smaller than me. Actually, he's the smallest boy in the class. He makes up for his small body with a big brain, though. He's into gadgets and computers and math. And he *loves* chess. Which is cool, because it means I don't have to go to chess club with Izzy. It also means that they're good friends, too, so the three of us hang out together a lot.

Anyway. Izzy had gotten a notebook out of her bag, opened it, and written — and underlined — the date in the top right-hand corner.

Izzy likes to do things properly.

"Let's start with a list," she said. "Or maybe a flowchart." She smiled. "Yes, a flowchart. That'll be fun."

"My limbs are disappearing, one by one, and you think we could describe this as fun?"

"Absolutely! Once we've established why it's happening, you just need to figure out how to harness it so you can control when it happens."

"Oh! Is that *all*? Why didn't you say so earlier?"

"Come on, think about it. You've got a superpower!"

I laughed. "Superpower? I wouldn't exactly call it —"

"Jess, you can turn invisible! What's that if it's not a superpower?"

"Well . . . OK, I guess."

Izzy grinned. "See! And once you've learned how to control it, who knows what you could do? You could go around the world doing good deeds. You could be a superhero!"

"Whoa! Hold on. Let's take it a step at a time, OK?"

"OK," Izzy agreed. Then she added something that made me feel better about the whole thing. And reminded me why she was my best friend. "You won't ever be on your own with this," she said. "I'll be with you every step of the way. I'm going to help you figure it out. Whatever happens, it'll all be OK. OK?"

I nodded. I didn't trust my voice.

"And once we've gotten to the bottom of it, we're going to have some fun," she went on. "And maybe do some slightly superhero-type stuff, too."

I thought about what she was saying. Perhaps she was right. If I could somehow learn to control this thing, make myself invisible whenever I wanted to, then perhaps we *could* have some fun with it. *And* perhaps I could do a good deed here and there.

Izzy was scribbling in the notebook. I read over her shoulder. "'Slightly Superhero Strategy'?"

Izzy shrugged. "It'll work for now."

I took the notebook from her and scribbled some notes of my own.

Step One: Find out why this is happening.
Step Two: Learn how to control it.
Step Three: Use power to do good.
Step Four: Have some fun.

"See?" Izzy said with a smile. "You're thinking like a slightly superhero already."

Chapter 3

I opened my laptop again and pulled a second chair over to my desk.

Izzy sat down next to me. "What are we doing?" she asked.

"Step One." I opened a search engine. I stopped for a moment while I thought about how to word it, then I typed "turning invisible" into the search bar.

"Whoa!" Izzy exclaimed as we stared at the screen. There were 57,843,521 results. "Where on earth do we start?"

I shrugged. "With the first one?"

I clicked on the first link. It took us to a page called "How to Become Invisible." Not strictly necessary, as I'd already done that part. But maybe it would tell me if there was something I'd done without realizing.

The page talked about advanced camouflage methods, as used in James Bond films. I didn't exactly feel like an international superspy, so we moved on to the next link, "Being Invisible: Tips and Techniques."

"This says it takes a lot of mental effort to do it. That doesn't seem right. I wasn't even trying," I said after reading a few paragraphs.

"Hmm. Maybe the writer uses a different method," Izzy said.

I stared at her. "A different method from what? I don't *have* a method."

"OK, look. He's explaining how to do it."

We read the instructions. Basically, I had to close my eyes, imagine my body becoming transparent, repeat the word "invisible" silently to myself over and over again, and get my "invisibuddy"— aka Izzy—to write down as a percentage how visible I was.

"I think you'd know about it if you had been visualizing yourself becoming transparent and saying the word 'invisible' over and over again," Izzy pointed out. She was right. We moved on.

21

"Forget about the how-to ones," I said as we scrolled down. "We don't need to know *how* to do it. We need to know *why*."

"Good plan," Izzy agreed. We scanned the list.

"How about that one?" Izzy pointed to a title halfway down the screen.

"'Incredible accounts of people who suddenly became completely invisible,'" I read out loud. "Sounds promising." I clicked on the link.

We read the first paragraph together.

A woman named Melanie in Ventura, California, had a strange experience while sitting on her own living-room sofa. While just staring at the wall, she became, she believes, invisible. Her husband walked around the house looking for her. He even walked right by her, just a few feet away, and did not see her. The episode lasted about ten minutes, then suddenly she was visible again.

I looked at Izzy.

"You've gone white," she said.

At least I haven't gone invisible, I thought.

We read on. There were several accounts of people who discovered that they had become invisible. It never lasted long, and they'd had no warning. It just happened—generally when they were at a party where they felt they were being ignored. To be honest, I wasn't convinced by the stories. Neither was I terribly convinced by the scientist who had apparently invented something he called an Electro-Helmet. He put the helmet on, stepped inside a closet, touched some "contact gloves" on the ceiling, and—presto!—when he came out of the closet, he was invisible!

"I saw someone do something like that in a magic show once," Izzy said.

"Exactly. This is a magician's trick, not someone who goes invisible without knowing why or how."

We clicked on page after page. We read about witches' brews and invisibility paint; we watched videos of people fading away, pickpockets stealing purses without being noticed—in other words, a bunch of phonies, cronies, and criminals.

"This isn't getting us anywhere," I said with a sigh.

Izzy picked up the pad. "I agree. Look, why don't we forget about Step One for now and move on to Step Two?"

"Learn how to control it?"

Izzy nodded.

"How are we supposed to do that?"

"I haven't figured that out yet."

We sat in silence for a while. Then I had a thought. "How about I go through all the things I did and felt as I was falling asleep and you make a list? Then perhaps I can try to do all the same things, but without going to sleep."

Izzy's eyes widened. "Jessica, you're a genius. That could work."

I thought about the process. "OK, so I guess I closed my eyes first of all."

"Closed eyes," Izzy repeated, scribbling on the pad.

"Then I felt sleepy."

"Felt sleepy."

"I think my heart rate probably slowed down a bit."

"Heart rate slowed," Izzy repeated.

I thought about what else I'd felt. "I think that's all."

Izzy finished scribbling and looked up. "So we've got closed eyes, felt sleepy, and heart rate slowed. Anything else?"

I shook my head. "Can't think of anything."

Izzy chewed the end of her pen. "Nothing at all?"

I thought a bit more. "Wait! That's it!" I said.

"That's what?"

"Nothing at all! I was thinking about nothing. Maybe that's the thing I have to do. Empty my mind. Think about nothing. Perhaps that's how I go invisible!"

Izzy stopped chewing her pen. "Try it," she said. "Can't do any harm."

I lay on the bed and closed my eyes. *Think about nothing, think about nothing.*

The problem was, the more I tried to think about nothing, the more I realized how full of thoughts my mind actually was. There were thoughts in every nook and cranny of my brain, whizzing around so quickly I couldn't even catch them and tell what they were, never mind stop them. My brain felt like the fast lane on the highway. Geography lesson. Rock formation. Homework. Worries about turning invisible. Questions about why it might be happening.

"Try to relax." Izzy's voice filtered through the fast lane.

Try to relax? Sure! I bet everyone who's just discovered that they can turn invisible feels really relaxed.

The thoughts whizzed by even faster.

25

Then I had an idea. I pictured each thought as a car on the highway, speeding by. As each car zoomed past, I imagined it going off into the distance and disappearing over the horizon. I did it over and over, until, after a while, there were no more cars. My mind had gone blank.

"It's happening!" Izzy squealed.

My eyes flicked open. "Really?"

Izzy pointed at my foot. "It started there about ten seconds ago. It's stopped now."

"Izzy, we were right," I breathed. "I just have to empty my mind and I turn invisible."

Izzy looked at me, a sparkle in her eyes. "Come on," she said. "Let's practice. See how much of you we can get to disappear."

I met her eyes. Did I really want to do this? What if I disappeared altogether? What if I never came back?

My head was full of questions again. But that was the whole point. All I had right now were questions, and we needed some answers.

"OK," I said, lying down again and closing my eyes. "Let's do it."

Chapter 4

We spent half the evening practicing. Every time I managed it, Izzy let out a shrieking squeal of excitement and broke me out of my concentration with a start. After a while, she managed to control her squealing and I managed to control my mind and something began to change. Once we'd been working on it for about two hours, I found I could even open my eyes without affecting my invisibility.

"Izzy, look!" I said. I was staring down at my body. Correction: I was staring at my shoulders, which were hovering in the air with a big, blank, me-size space below them.

Izzy clapped. "That's amazing! Now see if you can do it without closing your eyes at all."

I took a breath, kept my eyes open, and did the thing with the cars disappearing over the horizon, leaving an open space behind them. It was like I sectioned off a part of my mind and emptied it out while keeping the rest of me functioning at the same time.

My toes and fingertips tingled softly, as though someone were gently pouring sand over them. I watched them disappear. Then my arms and legs went. Soon, my entire body had vanished. But I was still there. I could see Izzy, staring at me — or at the space where I'd been a moment ago.

I reached into the empty part of my mind and switched it back on. As I did, my body came back into focus.

Izzy took her glasses off and rubbed them. Then she put them back on and let her breath out in a whistle. "That was quite something," she said.

I nodded. "It totally was." My mind was far from empty now. It was filling with a hundred ideas. The fun we could have, the mischief we could get into. The stunts I could pull.

"Know what?" I said. "I think I'm starting to like this invisibility thing."

We practiced for another hour or so, until I could switch the invisibility on and off at will and still see, talk, and even walk around the room. That was the most fun: creeping up behind Izzy and tapping her on the shoulder when she thought I was sitting in front of her.

We had a bit of a close call at one point. Mom came up while I was invisible. "Come on, girls, it's way past bedtime. Time to—" She stopped. Looked around the room. "Where's Jessica?" she asked.

"Um. She's . . . she's, er, in the bathroom," Izzy stammered.

At which point, I sneaked silently past Mom—making sure not to brush against her. I was invisible, after all, not un*tou*chable. Then I ran along the landing and into the bathroom, carefully pulled the door closed, flushed the toilet, turned myself visible again, and ambled back toward my bedroom just as Mom was turning back onto the landing.

"There you are," she said.

"Oh, hi, Mom," I said casually.

"I was just telling Isobel that I think it's lights-out time. It's nearly midnight!"

"You're right. We've been working pretty hard," I said. "I'm tired."

Mom kissed my head as she passed me. "You're such good girls," she said.

I bit my lip. I felt a little guilty, but mostly I felt excited. I couldn't wait to start practicing my new superpower out in the real world.

The next morning, I was awake early. I leaned over in bed to see Izzy in her sleeping bag on the blow-up mattress, reading a book.

"You're awake," I said.

"Couldn't sleep."

"Me neither."

I jumped out of bed. "Come on, then," I said. "Let's get going."

An hour later, we were showered, dressed, breakfasted, and ready to catch the first bus into town.

Mom came to the door with us. She was wearing exercise clothes. Mom works up at the rec center. She manages the reception desk and runs a few classes, too. Saturday is Dance for the Over-50s.

"Have a lovely day," she said. "Don't be back late."

"We won't," I called as we skipped down the driveway.

Half an hour later, we stepped off the bus and

walked along the main street. Izzy stopped outside our town's one and only department store.

I stopped beside her. "Bertram's? What are we doing here?"

"It's the busiest shop on a Saturday morning. Might be a good place to test your powers in public for the first time."

I looked in the window. It was full of mannequins dressed in all sorts of different outfits. I suddenly had an idea for how we could make it fun.

We wandered around the store for a bit. Once I had located the best spots for our first public experiment, I grabbed a couple of sweaters off a rack. "I'll go and try these on," I said.

Izzy nodded. "So you can make yourself invisible in the changing rooms."

"Exactly. Not advisable in the middle of a busy department store."

The woman at the desk handed me a tab without even looking at me. "Cubicle number eight," she said in a bored voice.

As soon as I was in the changing room, I hung the sweaters up, sectioned off a bit of my mind, made it go blank, and waited.

A minute later, I was invisible! My stomach

tingled with a whisper of anxiety as I slipped out of the changing rooms. What if I couldn't keep it up with all these people around? What if I got so distracted I became visible again without realizing and someone saw it happen?

I shook my head. No. I'd be fine. And, anyway, that's what we were here for. If I was going to become so expert at using my power that I was going to do good with it one day, I'd have to start somewhere, and a department store on a Saturday morning was as good a place as any.

Izzy was waiting just outside the changing rooms. I sidled up to her. "Hey, Izzy," I whispered.

Izzy jumped. "Jess, is that you?" she hissed.

"Er, no, it's the other person who has just turned invisible and also happens to know your name," I said. "Of course it's me! Come on, let's go."

Beside the changing rooms, a pair of mannequins faced each other. A man and a woman. The man was dressed in a suit, the woman in a soft flowing dress. Before doing anything else, I touched one of the mannequins to double-check it didn't turn invisible. It didn't. Good. It was definitely just me and my clothes that disappeared. OK, time to have some fun.

"Watch this," I whispered to Izzy.

I raised the female mannequin's arm up to her mouth before letting out a huge sneeze.

A woman walking past with a stroller nearly jumped out of her skin. A man in a suit hurrying by said, "Bless you," without breaking his stride. A couple of young girls just stared. Izzy guffawed.

I looked around the store. "I've got another one," I said. We headed over to the sportswear department and I took my place behind a female mannequin wearing a tennis outfit.

A few minutes later, two bored-looking teenage boys were heading toward me, both wearing low-slung jeans and baggy T-shirts. One of them was lanky and tall; the other was shorter, with an acne-covered face and a backward baseball cap.

I cleared my throat and put on a super girlie voice.

"Hey, guys, does my butt look big in this?" I asked.

The two boys stared at the mannequin. The tall one turned bright red and clammed up.

The one in the cap tried to speak: "Umm, do you, does your, did you . . . ?" he said.

"I said, does my butt look big in this?" I repeated. This time I even moved the mannequin's arm so she was pointing at her little tennis skirt.

The tall boy turned to his friend. "The . . . the . . ." he said, pointing at the mannequin.

"Yeah," his friend replied.

They both stared, openmouthed, at the mannequin for another couple of moments. Then, at the same time, they both suddenly remembered they were supposed to be cool and pulled themselves together.

"Obviously a marketing stunt," the cap boy said.

"Didn't fool me for a second," the other one agreed as they turned around and walked away.

"We should get out of here," I whispered to Izzy. "Or someone's going to catch us."

We made our way out of the store and ran around the corner into a deserted alleyway, where I turned myself visible again.

Izzy had tears streaming from her eyes. "That was so funny!" she said. "Did you see those boys actually check out the mannequin's butt?" She burst out laughing all over again. "This is too much fun."

"Come on," I said. "Let's go to the town center and see what else we can do."

Over the next hour, I discovered I had a

particular affinity with pets. One little boy had quite a lengthy conversation with his dog, as though it were the most normal thing in the world to discuss the latest computer games with a Yorkshire terrier.

My favorite moment was when I knelt next to a German shepherd, and, in a deep voice, politely asked when the next bus was due. Then all twenty people waiting at the bus stop turned, as one, to stare at the dog. It was the way he stared back at them that cracked me up. His expression seemed to say, "Yes, I did ask about bus times. You have a problem with that?"

Unfortunately, the dog didn't actually say that, because I was laughing too much to make him say anything at that point.

I even managed to do something slightly superhero-y.

We were cutting through Bertram's to get back to the town center. As we passed the jewelry department, I spotted a little girl checking out a stand of watches while her mom talked to a shop assistant.

"Mommy, I like this one!" the girl said, holding up a watch with a hefty price tag.

Her mom didn't even look up. "Annabelle,

leave the watches alone! If you break one of those, you'll be paying for it in allowance for the next ten years," she said, and went back to her conversation.

I watched Annabelle put the watch back in its box. The only trouble was, she didn't put it in correctly, and as she raised her hand to hook it back on the stand, the watch slipped out of the box.

Without stopping to think, I bent down and caught the watch, a millisecond before it would have smashed to pieces on the floor.

Still invisible, I stood up and placed it carefully back in Annabelle's hand. The girl gazed at the watch in her palm, her mouth open. Then she glanced at her mom—who was still talking to the shop assistant. Without missing a beat, she quickly reached up and, more carefully this time, put the watch back in its box.

A decade's worth of allowance stayed intact. Perhaps a young girl's belief in magic did, too.

And I had done my first heroic deed.

❖

We had come out the other end of Bertram's and were heading back through the square when we spotted a crowd of people.

Wondering what was going on, we squeezed our way through the crowd, until we were stopped from going any farther by a thick rope and some security guards in front of the Penbridge Hotel.

"What's happening?" Izzy asked.

"Hang on. I'll find out." I glanced around to check that no one was looking. All eyes were fixed firmly on the hotel doors, so I quickly turned myself invisible. Then I slipped under the rope and went right up to the hotel doors to see what all the fuss was about.

Two people were coming out of the hotel. Instantly, the crowd started roaring and holding out books and photos for them to sign.

I recognized the couple right away. Andy and Celia Fairhurst—one of those athlete-marries-model celebrity clichés. What on earth were they doing in Penbridge? Other than standing on the hotel steps flashing toothy grins at the crowd?

Actually, I didn't really care what they were doing here. They'd been on *Celebrity Marriage Wars* last year and had come across as the rudest, nastiest, and most unpleasant couple in the world. Why people were crowding around to get their autographs I had no idea.

I slipped past and headed back to the crowd.

Just when I was almost near enough to touch them, and blinking in the glare of all the cameras flashing as everyone took pics of the celebrity couple, I was suddenly overcome with an urge to tell them what I thought of them.

Obviously, I was invisible, not un*hear*able — and with so many people around I didn't want to get caught — so I did the next best thing. I stuck my tongue out at them.

I mean, it wasn't as if anyone could see me do it, right?

Chapter 5

Wrong.

It was at approximately half past seven on Monday morning, as I was in the process of washing down two slices of toast and marmalade with a swig of orange juice and sitting opposite Dad as he read the newspaper, that I discovered quite *how* wrong I'd been. And quite how visible!

Andy and Celia were pictured in full-color glory on the front page of our local paper.

Directly behind them, thumb on nose, fingers waggling in a childish wave and tongue sticking out, so was I.

To be fair, the main focus of the picture was the happy couple, and I was completely blurry behind them. If I was lucky, no one would even recognize me. But *I* recognized me—and someone who knew me well might recognize me, too! How had it happened? I'd been invisible at the time. Hadn't I?

I didn't have time to ponder any more questions. I had about three seconds to do something. Dad was holding the paper up in front of him. Luckily, in his opinion the most important news is what's happening with the local sports teams, so he always starts with the back page. But his fingers were starting to twitch. Any second now he would turn the newspaper over and see me—possibly.

I wasn't prepared to take the risk. Dad runs a real estate agency in town and is vice president of the Penbridge Chamber of Commerce. He's always telling me this means it's important for us to set a good example. To whom, I'm not sure. I'm also not sure what difference it makes to him selling houses if I get into trouble from time to time. (Which I do. Quite a bit.) But, either way, he'd go crazy if he saw me sticking my tongue out at celebrities. Plus, how on earth would I explain it?

I thought quickly, and then I did the only possible thing I could do. I leaned across the table and knocked my orange juice over.

It flooded the table and, more important, it caught the front page of the *Penbridge Chronicle*.

"Dad, watch out!" I screamed, jumping up and grabbing the newspaper off him as I did. While he was busy leaping off his chair and looking down at his pants to make sure they were dry, I gave the newspaper a quick rub in the orange juice, just to be on the safe side.

"Jessica, you clumsy thing," Dad said. "Look what you've done to my paper."

I looked at the sodden newspaper. "Dad, I'm *so* sorry," I said with a crestfallen frown. "I'll go out and buy you a new one." It was a gamble, but I had to sound sincere.

Dad looked at his watch. "It doesn't matter," he said. "There's never much of interest in that local rag anyway."

"True," I agreed as I took the soggy paper to the trash can.

"Well, it's obvious what happened," Izzy said at break time after I told her what I'd seen.

"It is?" Only Izzy could say that anything about someone turning invisible and then appearing in their local newspaper was obvious. She'd probably read about it in a book or something.

"I read about it in a book," she went on. "Someone was invisible, and—oh, wait. No, I think they were a ghost, actually."

"Right," I said, feeling better by the minute.

Izzy carried on. "You couldn't see them in real life, but they could be seen in photographs—and by animals as well, I think. Maybe that's what happens when you're invisible, too."

"Maybe," I agreed. It made about as much sense as anything else. And it would also explain why some of the dogs I'd invisibly crouched beside on Saturday had wagged their tails the whole time I was there.

"So we need to be careful of that from now on."

"Agreed," I said. "Meanwhile, let's just hope no one else spots the idiot in the *Penbridge Chronicle*."

"Don't worry about it. Hardly anyone reads the local paper. And even if they do, like you said, it was totally blurred. I bet you and I are the only ones who'd even know it was you."

Which wasn't exactly the reply I'd been looking for. Something more along the lines of "You're not an idiot at all" would have been nice. But at least she was right. I was probably safe—for now.

"Iz, do you think we're ever going to get to the bottom of this?" I asked.

Izzy chewed the edge of her little finger. "I don't know. I spent last night doing more searches online but couldn't find anything. I don't know what else we can do."

"Me neither," I agreed. "It makes my head hurt to think about it." I thought back to the notes we'd made for the Slightly Superhero Strategy, and how it had felt good to keep that girl out of trouble in the department store. "Why don't we think about Step Three?" I suggested.

"Step Three?" Izzy asked.

"Of the strategy. The one about doing good," I reminded her. "I think I might have an idea."

We spent the rest of break discussing my idea. It was a combination of Steps Three and Four, actually. It was about having fun, but also a way of doing something for which I was fairly sure every student in the school—and possibly a fair number of the teachers—would be thankful.

The idea: Operation Principal's Office.

Like any other perfect plan, Operation Principal's Office was simple. Mr. Bell is one of those principals who like everyone to know how open and approachable they are, so he keeps his office door open almost all the time. Which makes it easy for an invisible person — aka me — to go in and out pretty much anytime they like.

The plan was that I would wait till he had stepped out, and I would step *in* and send an e-mail to all the staff — from him — informing them that there was to be an inspection of the school's plumbing system on Friday, and as a result, they were to tell all their students that school would finish at lunchtime.

I think you'll agree that this plan was genius. Plus, it was a very special gift from me to Izzy, as a thank-you for her support. We had a geography test on Friday afternoon, and Izzy was dreading it. She'd been so busy being freaked out by my turning invisible last week that she hadn't listened to a word of the lesson. If Operation Principal's Office went according to plan, she'd get an extra week to study.

We decided we would put the plan into action on Thursday. That gave us a few days to scope out Mr. Bell's movements and pick the best time. It also gave me a few days to try to build up the courage to do one of the most daring things I had ever done. I tried not to think about the possibility of getting caught and instead focused on the idea of giving the entire student body a whole extra half a day of weekend.

Because, surely, that was the most important thing.

On Wednesday evening, Mom popped her head around my bedroom door. "Jess, can you come and set the table? Nancy will be here any minute."

I put my homework away and went down to help Mom. Nancy is a midwife at the hospital. In fact, she's the midwife who delivered me. That's how she and Mom met. They'd kept in touch ever since. She was Mom's best friend now, and she came over for dinner at least once a week.

Nancy's cool. She's tall and funky and wears her hair tied back in long dreadlocks. She's not like most other adults. She's always interested in me and acts more like an aunt than a friend of my mom's. She even gives me presents for birthdays and Christmas.

Like a couple of weeks earlier, when I turned thirteen, she gave me a beautiful necklace with a tiny heart made out of rose quartz. I hadn't taken it off yet. Even at school, where you're not allowed to wear jewelry, I kept it on under my uniform. It was beautiful, and typical of Nancy to buy such a lovely gift.

The doorbell rang. "Jess, can you get that?" Mom called from the kitchen.

I went to let Nancy in. She was wearing skinny jeans and a T-shirt that said in large letters, KEEP CALM AND BE ALERT. Underneath, in smaller letters, it said, YOUR COUNTRY NEEDS LERTS. As always, she gave me a big smile and a bigger hug. "How's my favorite teenager?"

"Hungry. You're late," I replied, smiling back.

Nancy laughed as we went into the kitchen.

"Thank goodness you're here," Dad said, reaching into the wine cupboard. "I've got an excuse to open a bottle of red now."

"Oh, go on, then, if you insist," she said as he passed her a glass. "Luckily for me, Jean asked if I can swap shifts, so I don't work till tomorrow afternoon."

"Excellent," Dad said. "Better make it a large one, then."

"Dinner," Mom said, and we all sat down and ate, talked, and laughed for the next hour.

After we'd washed up, Dad went to watch a documentary about house renovations that he'd recorded from the night before, I went upstairs to do my homework, and Mom and Nancy stayed in the kitchen, talking.

At one point, I went down to get my pencil case. As soon as I came into the room, they stopped talking quite abruptly and both looked at me guiltily.

"You talking about me?" I asked, half joking.

"Of course not, darling," Mom said quickly, her face reddening as it always does when she's lying. "Why would we be talking about you?"

I left them to it but felt a bit odd. It was *obvious* they'd been talking about me, but why?

I had an idea. I'd give them a few minutes, then go back downstairs invisibly and find out what they were talking about.

I went back upstairs as noisily as I could, so they'd know the coast was clear and they could go back to their conversation.

I watched the clock. Two minutes later, I made myself invisible and crept downstairs as silently as I could.

"To be honest, I hadn't really noticed anything until you mentioned it," Mom was saying. "But now that I think about it, yes, she has been a bit different lately."

"Different how?" Nancy asked. She was leaning across the kitchen table and looking intensely at Mom. *Were* they talking about me?

"It's hard to explain," Mom said. She got up from the table to fetch the wine from the sideboard, nearly walking right into me. I dodged out of her path just in time. "I guess she's been a bit more secretive the last week or so. She and Isobel always seem to be discussing something privately and stop the minute I come in."

Er, hello? Pot calling kettle black at all, Mom?

"Any idea what they've been talking about?" Nancy asked.

Mom shook her head. "It's funny; on the one hand, it's as though it's something they're excited about, but on the other hand, I think Jessica's been looking worried, too."

"Worried?"

"I'm probably imagining it. Or you're putting ideas into my head." Mom shook her head. "I don't know. It's probably nothing. Only, now that you've asked me, I suppose I do think she's been behaving differently. Why? Do you think there's something wrong with her? What made you ask in the first place?"

"I was just interested. I'm sure she's fine,"

Nancy said quickly. Too quickly. Then in a super-bright voice, she changed the subject. "She seems to like the necklace I gave her."

"She loves it," Mom replied. "I haven't seen her take it off yet!"

"Really? Not at all?" Nancy asked lightly, although she leaned forward and stared into Mom's eyes as she spoke.

Mom leaned back a little. "Um. I don't think so. Why do you ask? Nance, you're being ever so strange this evening."

Nancy laughed her big belly laugh. "I am, aren't I?" she said. "It must be the wine, I expect. Sorry."

"Don't worry," Mom said. "I know you care about Jess."

"Almost like a daughter," she said. "She's the nearest thing I've got."

"I know. We're lucky to have you." Mom reached over and squeezed Nancy's hand. "Now, then, tell me the latest on that doctor who got caught in the supply closet with the new nurse."

Hospital gossip was beyond my level of interest. I crept out of the kitchen and back upstairs.

In my room, I tried to figure out what that whole conversation had been about. Why was

Nancy asking about me? How much of my recent behavior and antics had Mom been aware of? And why was Nancy suddenly so interested in whether I'd taken my necklace off?

For the first time in two weeks, I took it off and held it in my hands. It had almost become a lucky charm to me. But after eavesdropping on Mom and Nancy's conversation, I wasn't sure I still felt the same way about it.

I left the necklace on my nightstand and started my homework. Math. Quadratic equations. Which meant that after twenty minutes I was so bored I decided to have an early night instead.

I settled into bed. Within minutes I was fast asleep and dreaming about cliffs made out of rose quartz. The cliffs were collapsing, and I was in the middle of them. I was shouting out for help, but I was invisible and no one could see me, or hear me, either. The cliffs were falling, bright-red rose rocks tumbling down until, eventually, they lay all around me, trapping me inside a deep glowing well that I had no idea how to get out of. And where no one could ever find me because no one knew I was there.

The next morning, I woke sweating, restless, and late for school.

Mom was at my bedroom door. "Jess, get up!"

I had the quickest shower in the world, threw my school uniform on, and wolfed down a piece of toast in record time.

"See you tonight," I called, grabbing my bag and running out the door to catch the bus.

Izzy was waiting for me at the school entrance. "Today's the day," she said. "You sure you're up for this?"

"I have no idea," I said honestly. I mean, I'd never shied away from the occasional prank, but this was a whole new level. Could I really do it? *Should* I really do it? I wasn't sure. And could I actually get caught?

It was highly unlikely anyone would suspect that a student had turned invisible and sneaked into the principal's office! Plus, I owed it to Izzy and to all the other students, who I'd silently promised would have a long weekend.

We'd planned the operation for morning break time, when Mr. Bell would be in the staff room with the other teachers for about ten minutes. Plenty of time to turn invisible, sneak into his office, send a quick e-mail, and get out.

As soon as the bell rang, Izzy and I made a dash for the girls' bathroom nearest to his office. I almost walked into someone on the way through the door.

"Oops, sorry," I said automatically. Then I looked up. It was Heather Berry. She had a couple of her minions in tow, following behind her like obedient lapdogs.

For a millisecond, Heather's eyes met mine. They looked different from usual. They didn't quite have their usual shiny confidence. They held my gaze, and just briefly, I thought Heather was actually going to speak to me. A second later, the minions caught up with her and she sniffed, stuck her nose up as usual, and turned away.

As she turned, she pulled her bag over her shoulder and I noticed something on her hand. A ring. I'd never seen that before. It was bright yellow and flashed in the light from the corridor. I don't know why, but it made me catch my breath.

A moment later, Heather and her minions had gone. Before they rounded the corner at the end of the corridor, Heather turned quickly back to me and—well, I was probably imagining it, but I think she might have smiled. She was probably just sharing a secret joke about us, as usual.

"Snobby socks," Izzy said under her breath.

"Ignore her," I said. "She's not worth it. Come on." I headed toward one of the stalls and put Heather and her minions and her super-flash ring out of my mind. I locked the door behind me, then took a few slow breaths. *Think about nothing,* I told myself, and waited for my body to disappear.

I gave it a minute, then opened my eyes. I was still there! What was going on? I'd become pretty smooth at it after nearly a week of practicing, but for some reason, it wasn't happening. Probably the nerves.

I tried again. Closing my eyes, I tried to clear my mind. *Nothing, nothing, nothing.*

It still didn't work. What was wrong? Why wasn't anything happening?

"Are you ready?" Izzy's voice hissed through the toilet door.

"Two minutes," I hissed back. *Try harder. Breathe. Relax.*

It didn't work.

"Come on, Jess." Izzy's voice again. "We're going to run out of time."

I took a long, slow breath, closed my eyes, and tried one final time.

Nothing.

I opened the stall door.

"At last," Izzy said, already halfway to the door. "Come on, we're—" Then she turned around and saw me. "Jess, you're . . ."

I nodded glumly. "I know."

"Have you changed your mind?"

"Not intentionally."

"What happened?"

I shrugged. "No idea."

Izzy was about to reply when a couple of tenth-grade girls came in. We slipped out of the bathroom and went outside. We passed Tom on the way. "Hey, guys," he said with a smile. "What are you up to?"

For a moment, I almost wanted to answer him honestly. I mean, this was Tom. He was virtually like a brother to me and a best friend to Izzy. If anyone could be trusted to share all this weirdness, it was Tom. And, actually, if anyone had a brain wired up in the right way to have bright ideas about what was going on, it was probably Tom, too.

I opened my mouth to reply.

Then I thought about what I might say. "Well, we were planning to do this trick where I turn invisible and then pretend to be the principal and send an e-mail to the entire school—but for some reason, it went wrong."

Yeah. Not sure that would go down too well.

"We, er, well . . . nothing much," I said in the end.

Tom nodded. "See you at chess tonight, Izzy?"

Izzy nodded and Tom left us to it. We headed over to our favorite spot in the school yard.

"So," Izzy said, once we were on our own, "why do you think it's not working?"

I had no answers, only guesses. "Maybe I was too nervous to empty my mind," I suggested.

"Maybe a bit of you knew it was wrong, and that part of you wouldn't let you do it."

"Huh?"

"Like when you get hypnotized," Izzy said. "You can't do anything under hypnosis that you wouldn't be prepared to do in real life." Both Izzy's parents were therapists, so she knew things like that. "Perhaps this works the same way."

"Could be," I said. "Or maybe I just can't do it anymore. Maybe whatever made me able to do it only lasted a short time, and now it's back to normal."

I couldn't help feeling sad at that thought. I mean, I knew that only a week earlier, the idea of turning invisible had completely freaked me out. But I'd gotten used to it now. I liked it.

Izzy shook her head. "I don't know. I just don't know," she said.

The bell rang for the end of break. "Look, come over tonight and we'll try it again," I said. "If it was just because I was nervous, I should be able to do it. If I can't, we'll know that it was something else and we can forget all about it."

Izzy picked up her bag and we headed back to class.

"Sounds like a plan," she said. "I'll be by after chess club. Oh, and I guess I'd better bring my geography stuff with me. We'll have to study now, after all."

Chapter 6

I sat up and opened my eyes for the fifth time. "Enough," I said with a sigh. "I can't do it anymore. Let's just accept it and be done with it."

"One more try," Izzy pleaded. "I'll watch more closely; see if you're doing anything different."

"I'm *not* doing anything different," I insisted. "I'm doing exactly the same thing I've done before, and it's not working. It's over."

Izzy ran a hand through her hair. "I don't get it," she said. "Why would it just stop like this? It's not logical."

Izzy loves things to be logical, loves theories and explanations. I could have pointed out that if we were going to get hung up on what was or wasn't logical, we might have to rethink the whole "turning invisible" thing altogether. I didn't, though. Partly because I didn't want to upset her and partly because when I got up off my bed, something caught my eye as it glinted in the setting sun.

My necklace.

The necklace I'd worn every day since my birthday, until yesterday. The one thing I could think of that I had done differently. I hadn't turned invisible since I'd taken it off.

Could the necklace have anything to do with it?

It was just a coincidence, surely. I mean, it wasn't possible. It was *ridiculous*. How could a piece of jewelry have anything to do with turning invisible?

Even so, without saying anything, I found myself reaching out for the necklace, putting it on, and closing my eyes.

"What are you doing?" Izzy asked. "I thought you'd given up on . . ."

Her voice trailed off as she let out a breath. And I knew why. I knew because when I looked down, what I saw took my breath away, too.

I had turned invisible.

"The necklace makes you go invisible," Izzy

said. When I became visible again, Izzy stared at the rose quartz dangling around my neck and shook her head. "That's, like, wow, I mean, that's . . ."

I knew what she meant, even if she hadn't actually managed to utter a complete sentence. "Yeah, it is," I said.

We checked and double-checked the theory. I took the necklace off and put it back on. Each time, without it, I couldn't turn invisible, and with it, I could. Then I had a thought. I unclasped the necklace and handed it to Izzy. "You try."

Izzy's eyes opened as wide as they might have if I'd handed her the crown jewels and suggested she try being queen for the day.

She took the necklace from me and fastened it around her neck. "What do I do?"

I laughed. "Come on, you've watched me do it about a thousand times. You know what to do by now. Close your eyes, relax, and clear your mind. Let's see if it works."

We spent about an hour trying to turn Izzy invisible. She tried the thing with the cars zooming over the horizon. She tried another one her mom had taught her for falling asleep—imagining fluffy clouds gliding across a big blue sky. She even tried counting sheep and turning her mind into a huge meadow. Nothing worked. Nothing even came close.

"Maybe you just haven't gotten the hang of it yet," I suggested as Izzy unclasped the necklace and took it off.

She shook her head. "My mind was as blank as that time the substitute teacher asked me the square root of 729. It couldn't have been any more empty if I'd been knocked unconscious." She handed me the necklace. "Whatever it is about this necklace and turning invisible, it only works for you."

I put the necklace back on, fastened it behind my neck, and slipped it under my clothes, out of sight, close to my skin.

"Where did it come from?" Izzy asked.

Which was when I realized I'd been avoiding thinking about that question. Nancy. She'd bought me the necklace.

And then I thought about the other thing I'd been avoiding thinking about. The conversation I'd overheard between Nancy and Mom.

Did Nancy know what the necklace could do? Was that possible? Surely Nancy would never spring something like that on me. Would she?

Several hours after Izzy had left, nearly bedtime, I left Mom and Dad watching *Supercook: The Final* and headed into the kitchen to make some hot chocolate. While I waited for the kettle to boil, I sat down and tried to put my thoughts into some sort of order.

My necklace enabled me to turn invisible. Nancy had given it to me. And then she had acted a bit strangely, asking my mom how I was and if I liked the gift. Was she just asking out of interest? I mean, surely it would be normal to ask if I liked a present she'd bought. Was it possible that she knew what it did? And how could I find out?

Well, obviously, I could ask her. *Hey, Nancy, don't suppose you know that the necklace you gave me has made me a superhuman freak who turns invisible, do you?* No, that wouldn't work. If she didn't know anything about it, her next conversation with Mom would probably include a discussion of the quickest way to get my head examined. And if she *did* know . . . Well, that thought freaked me out so much that I wasn't prepared to go there. Not yet. I needed more information first. But how to get it?

I went to get some milk for my cocoa. And that was when I spotted the magnetic reminder on the fridge. Tomorrow was the town's monthly recycling day. I suddenly had a thought.

The necklace had come wrapped up in some purple tissue paper stuck down with a label. I couldn't remember exactly what the label had said, but I knew it had writing on it, and I was pretty sure it was the name and address of the shop it had come from. If I could find that, perhaps I could track down where the necklace had come from without having to confront Nancy. And, given that a month's worth of our discarded paper was going to be taken away in the morning, tonight would be my only chance.

I could hear the *Supercook* closing theme song in the family room. Then Mom came into the kitchen. "All right, that's it. I'm calling it a night," she said, giving me a kiss.

"I'll be up in a minute," Dad replied as Mom headed up to their bedroom.

One down. Dad would probably spend another ten minutes channel surfing. He wouldn't be far behind her.

I'd go up to my own room, give them half an hour to get into bed and nod off, then all I had to do was go downstairs, sneak outside, rummage through a month's worth of recycling, find a tiny label on a scrunched-up piece of purple tissue paper that might or might not have the store's address on it, get that address, get back inside and up to bed, all without being found out.

Simple.

I could hear Dad snoring. I was listening outside the door. I couldn't hear Mom hissing at him to *stop* snoring, which meant she was probably asleep, too.

I tiptoed past, avoiding the squeaky floorboard, and crept downstairs. I sneaked across the hall, through the kitchen, and onto the back porch, where I carefully slid the bolt and slipped outside.

There was just about enough light from the streetlamp at the front of our house to see what I was doing. The recycling was in plastic bins at the side of the yard. I opened the first bin I saw. It was full of plastic bottles. Carefully pushing it aside, I moved on to the next one. Paper. Yes! I crouched down and began to rummage my way through four weeks' worth of cereal boxes, junk mail, packaging, newspapers, and magazines.

This wasn't going to be easy.

Eventually, I reached the bottom of the bin.

No tissue paper at all. I looked around. There were more bins. I opened a couple more. Cans in the first; glass in the second. Then I came to the final one, right in the corner of the yard. As soon as I opened the lid, the first thing I noticed was a whole bunch of "happy birthday" wrapping paper. Bingo!

I rummaged through the wrapping paper. *Come on, come on, it must be here somewhere.* I was starting to get a cramp from crouching down next to the bin when I spotted it. Tissue paper! Scrunched up into a ball inside a piece of wrapping paper. I opened it up and studied it as well as I could in the dim light. Yes! A label! I ripped off the label and shoved it in my pocket. Then I straightened my legs and went to stand up. Only, I lost my balance and fell onto the bin behind me, which I'd piled on top of another one. Unfortunately, I hadn't stacked it properly, and it fell with a clatter, tin cans spilling everywhere.

Nooooooooo!

I held my breath again and listened. Nothing. I was safe. I just needed to—

Wait. A light had come on in the kitchen. Someone was coming. I didn't have time to run away, and the bins were too small for me to hide behind. There was only one thing I could do. I closed my eyes, cleared my mind, and turned invisible.

"Hello?" Dad was standing in the back doorway in his pajamas, his hair sticking up in a sleepy mop. He was holding a rolling pin. "Who's there? I know there's someone out there. You'd better show your-self or there'll be trouble."

If I hadn't been so concerned with making sure Dad didn't notice me, I might have laughed. I mean, did he really think any serious burglar would be afraid of a middle-aged guy in striped pajamas trying to sound tough as he stood yawn-ing in the doorway with a rolling pin in his hand?

"I'm warning you." Dad raised his voice and held the rolling pin a bit higher. I crouched low and focused hard on keeping myself invisible. I mean, I know he wasn't exactly scary in his PJs and hold-ing a kitchen utensil, but I wasn't a hardened crim-inal and Dad was never in a good mood if he was woken up. Plus, I wasn't sure I'd be able to come up with a decent explanation for why I was crouched down among the recycling bins in the middle of the night.

And then, just as I was starting to get a cramp in my knees and wondering how long this standoff was going to last, something wonderful happened.

The neighbor's cat, Monty, leaped across the fence into our yard.

Dad jumped so hard he dropped the rolling pin. Then he peered into the darkness. "Monty, is that you?"

Monty skipped over to the shed next to the back door. Dad stepped out to pick him up. Monty purred like a motorcycle engine and rubbed his head against Dad's chest.

Dad tickled Monty under his chin. "Darn cat. You had us worried for a minute there. Darn Christine, too, forgetting to lock the back door," he said. "All right, be off with you, now. I'm going back to bed. And, unlike Christine, I'll lock the door behind me. What do you think, Monts? That a good idea?"

Which was when I realized I had to act fast. If I didn't get into the house before Dad, and he locked the door behind him, it could be a long, dark, cold night for me out here in the backyard.

Dad was still tickling Monty's neck. I seized the moment. Extricating myself from the bins with a light-footedness a ballerina would be proud of,

I tiptoed across the yard, edged past Dad, and zipped through the back door, seconds before Dad bent down to put Monty on the ground. With a final pet of the cat's head, he turned and came back in the house.

I was halfway across the kitchen as I heard him close the door behind him. I ran upstairs as quickly and as quietly as I could, crept into my bedroom, and finally let out the breath I'd been holding since I'd made a dash for the back door.

I listened as he crossed the landing and closed his bedroom door behind him. Only then did I feel safe to put on my bedside light and pull the label out of my jeans pocket. I held it up to the light.

Tiger's Eye, it said in a fancy, swirly font. That must be the name of the shop where my necklace had come from. There was an address under the name — 132 Beacon Street, Penbridge.

My heart took a leap. I didn't recognize the address or the shop name, but at least it was in Penbridge. It couldn't be too far away.

It took me hours to fall asleep after that. My mind wouldn't switch off. All I could think was that maybe Izzy and I could go to Tiger's Eye over the weekend. And that perhaps it would finally lead us to some answers.

Chapter 7

On Saturday morning, I was at Izzy's before she was even dressed. I waited for her to wolf down her breakfast and throw on some clothes, then I dragged her out of the house.

I'd checked out the route on my computer before leaving home, and I ran it by Izzy as we walked up to the bus stop at the end of her road. "We get the number seventeen into town and get off at the Memorial Gardens. Then we hang a left up Waterloo Road, and Beacon Street should be the third on our right."

Half an hour later, we were turning onto a long street with houses at each end and a row of stores in between; Beacon Street.

Tiger's Eye was right in the middle. We stopped outside and peered in. The window was filled with glass cases of jewelry, shelves of wooden animal ornaments, and colorful silk scarves. A smell that I recognized as incense wafted out onto the street, together with a tinkly tune that might have been panpipes.

I looked at Izzy and swallowed. "I'm nervous."

"Me too," Izzy replied. "But we're here now. And, anyway, what's the worst that can happen?"

I was fairly certain that the worst that could happen would be someone in the store instantly realizing that I was some kind of superhuman superfreak, kidnapping me, locking me in a dungeon, and experimenting on me for the rest of my life.

I didn't say any of that, though. Instead I shrugged and tried for a smile.

"Come on." Izzy pushed the door open, jangling a wind chime on the other side. I followed her in.

Inside, the shop was quite small. Cabinets and shelves lined every wall, all of them packed tightly with crystals and necklaces, bracelets, and animal ornaments that looked as if they'd come from every country in the world.

The shopkeeper was tall and wiry, with glasses perched so far down his nose I was surprised they stayed on. He was sitting on a stool behind the front counter, muttering to himself as he shuffled through paperwork. "Now, then, where did I put the . . . ? Ah, hmm, it was here before, and now it's . . . hmm. Well, I never . . ."

I coughed gently. The man looked up. He pushed his glasses up his nose and squinted. Looking from me to Izzy and back again, he nodded briskly.

"Yes?" he said. "Can I help you?"

Which was when I realized that we hadn't actually discussed what we were going to do once we got here. We stared silently back at him for a moment. Then I pulled myself together. If I didn't want him to get suspicious of me, it was probably a good idea to stop acting weird.

"We were wondering if you have any crystals we could look at." Great. It wasn't exactly hard to see that he had an entire shop full of crystals.

The man opened his arms to encompass the shop. "One or two," he said.

"Rose quartz, in particular," I went on, holding my breath. Why did I say that? He was *bound* to know why we were here now!

"Our most popular crystal," he drawled.

"Really?" Izzy stepped forward. "A friend of ours bought some from here recently."

The man seemed to be stifling a yawn as he continued to shuffle papers. "I'm not surprised. Rose quartz looks pretty and, you know, roses, romance, and all that."

"Maybe you'd remember our friend?" Izzy continued.

"I probably won't, actually," the man replied. "The number of customers I get in here, there's no way I can keep track of them all."

I looked around the empty shop. *Seriously?*

He stopped what he was doing and looked up. "What does this person look like?" he asked.

"Well, she's tall with a smiley face. She usually has her hair tied back and it's kind of long and dreadlocky," I said.

The man frowned and went back to his paperwork.

"And she wears odd clothes."

He looked up. "Oh, hold on a second. I think I *might* remember her. She was wearing a long yellow cardigan with a kilt with a pair of green tights."

That sounded like Nancy. In fact, I was sure of it. I knew the cardigan he meant. It also had pink flowers on it, but I didn't point that out.

"That's her!" I said.

"Came in twice, actually," the man went on. "First time on her own, then she came back the next day with a man."

With a man? I didn't know Nancy had a boyfriend. I made a mental note to find out more the next time she came for dinner.

"In fact, I couldn't tell you much about her, but I remember the man very clearly," the shopkeeper continued. "We had a long conversation about the crystals. He wanted to know all about which ones I had, where they came from, who my suppliers were — all sorts of things. He was a very good customer. The kind you want to look after. He bought a huge boxful of crystals. Said he wanted one of every single type that I had. Paid cash as well." He shuffled through his paperwork again. "In fact, now that I think about it, he was *particularly* interested in the rose quartz."

My heart leaped into my mouth. I tried to squeeze a few words around it. "Did he say where he was from?" I asked in a squeak.

The shopkeeper frowned again. "Actually, he left his business card." He pulled out a card from underneath a pile of receipts and waved it vaguely at us before dropping it back on the pile. I couldn't see what it said.

Izzy was peering at the card. She reached inside her bag and pulled out her notebook and pen. Then she glanced at me and gave me a quick nod. I knew what she was thinking. We needed this man's details. He might be our next clue. Someone showing that much interest in the rose quartz, and knowing Nancy— sure, it might all just be a coincidence, but right now it was the best lead we had.

I pretended to be interested in a huge wooden bird hanging from the ceiling on the other side of the shop. "I wonder if you could tell me about this," I asked, pointing at it.

The man's eyes brightened. "Ah, the eagle mobile. Now, this is a very special bird," he said, coming out from behind the counter and leading me across the shop. I followed him to the eagle and watched, feigning fascination, as he pulled on a hidden cord that lifted the bird's wings. Actually, it was very pretty. The way the wings rose and fell was so lifelike, it mesmerized me for a moment.

Then Izzy coughed and I remembered our mission. I glanced across the shop to see her putting her pen and notebook away in her bag. She must have noted down the necessary information.

"Well, thank you for your time," I said to the man. "It's a lovely shop and we'll come back again."

"Not buying anything?" he asked.

I felt guilty. Despite what he'd said, I got the feeling he hardly ever had any customers. I glanced at a basket full of random stones and crystals next to the register. It had a sign above it saying, SALE. EVERY ITEM IN THIS BASKET $2.50.

I rummaged around the basket, looking for something I liked. A couple of things caught my eye. A stone that reminded me of a beautiful pebble I'd found on vacation on a beach when I was about seven. It was bright turquoise with black squiggly lines running all over it. Another stone looked a bit like a Life Saver—white with gray splodges and a perfect hole in the center. The shopkeeper said it was called howlite.

"I'll take these, please," I said, pulling my purse out of my pocket. I handed him a five-dollar bill. Bye-bye, allowance.

He wrapped them both in tissue paper and stuck a label on them before handing them back to me.

I thanked the man and turned toward the door. It was time to get out of there.

We huddled in a café in Memorial Square with a couple of hot chocolates and studied the details that Izzy had scribbled down. There was an address and a phone number. The number was local; I didn't recognize the address: 33 Albany Road.

Izzy was busy tapping on her phone. After a minute, she held it up to show me the screen. There was a picture of a map with an X in the middle of it and Albany Road above it. At the bottom of the screen, it gave us various options for getting there. Six minutes by public transportation. Twenty-two minutes' walk.

We looked at each other. "What do you want to do?" Izzy asked.

My stomach suddenly seemed to be playing jump rope. We couldn't back out now, though. I took a last swig of my hot chocolate, wiped my mouth, and stood up. "Let's walk," I said. "I'm running out of money."

We discussed our next move as we made our way to Albany Road.

"So, what do we do when we get to this address?" Izzy asked.

I looked at her blankly. "Um," I said. "I don't really know." I thought about it. "Do we have his name?"

Izzy shook her head. "I think it was on the other side of the card, but I didn't dare turn it over in case the shopkeeper saw me and got angry with us."

I walked in silence for a minute as I thought a bit more.

"You're sure you don't want to just ask Nancy about this?" Izzy asked.

"Yes, I'm sure," I said quickly. Nancy had bought the necklace, but the shopkeeper had told us it was the man she'd brought in who had been most interested—particularly in the rose quartz. Plus, checking out some stranger whom I'd never met felt preferable to asking someone who was practically an aunt if she'd secretly set me up with something completely freaky and weird. "Let's stick to the mystery man," I said.

"Do you think he's going to be our guy?" Izzy asked. "Do you think he'll know what the crystal does?"

"No idea. But after what the man in the shop said, he seems like the best option."

Izzy smiled. "I hope so," she said.

The jump rope flipped around in my stomach. "Yeah," I said, trying to ignore the worried question marks spinning with it. "Me too."

Albany Road was a short cul-de-sac lined with small businesses. A few of them had names on them, like Evans Embroidery and Peters & Sons Fishing Equipment. Most were unnamed and looked anonymous and dark. All of them were closed and locked, some with shutters over the windows. The street felt silent and empty. And a little creepy.

We made our way down the road, glancing up at the doors to check the numbers. Number thirty-three was right at the end. This one had shutters, too — only these were open. It looked like someone was there.

Which was when I had a thought. I grabbed Izzy's arm. "Wait," I said. I nodded toward an alleyway between a couple of the buildings.

Izzy followed me into the alley. "What's up? You're not backing out?"

I shook my head. "Not at all. But we can't go over there without a plan. Come on, Izzy. When do you ever do *anything* without a plan?"

Izzy scrunched up her nose and fiddled with her glasses — orange with purple flecks in them today, to match her orange bag with purple writing. "You're right," she said. "So what do you suggest?"

I breathed out hard. "I think you need to go in there on your own," I said.

"You *are* backing out!"

"I'm not!"

"But you said—"

"I'll be with you," I interrupted. "But he won't know about it."

Izzy stared at me for a moment, then she smiled as she realized what I was getting at. "Because you'll be invisible!"

"It's the only way we'll actually find out anything," I told her. "What were we thinking we'd say? 'Oh, hi there. I don't suppose you've come across some crystals that make certain people turn invisible, have you? No? OK, sorry to have bothered you'? I mean, we'll never find out much by talking to him."

"You're going to go inside?"

I nodded. "You go to the door and distract him. I'll sneak in, have a look around, see if there's anything suspicious."

"Got it."

"Just don't go off and leave me, OK?"

" 'Course I won't go off and leave you. We're in this together, aren't we?"

"Hundred percent," I said. I decided not to

point out that Izzy wasn't the one who had to sneak invisibly into a mysterious building and creep around trying to find out what a scary stranger was up to. It wasn't her fault I was the only superfreak around here.

"Ready?" Izzy asked.

I looked around. The alleyway was deserted.

"As I'll ever be," I replied. I closed my eyes, cleared a section of my mind, and turned myself invisible.

"OK, let's go," I said, and we walked up to number thirty-three.

I stood back as Izzy pressed the doorbell. And then I held my breath while we waited to see who would come to the door.

Chapter 8

"Yes?" A man stood in the doorway and looked at Izzy. He was small and scruffy, his shirt half hanging out of baggy corduroys, a tie loosely done up, a pair of thick black-rimmed glasses halfway down his nose.

"Can I help you?" he asked. He wasn't exactly unfriendly—more impatient, as though we'd disturbed him from something important and he wanted to dispense with us and get back to it as quickly as he could.

He was standing right in the middle of the doorway. There was barely any space to see behind him, let alone squeeze past without him knowing. I could just about see a small and very sterile-looking hallway with a door leading into another room beyond.

What was in that room?

Izzy smiled innocently at the man. "I . . . er, I'm really sorry to bother you," she said. "I'm looking for number twenty-three."

"This is *thirty*-three," the man replied sharply.

"Oh, sorry, my mistake," Izzy replied as the man went to close the door.

I nudged her in the ribs to let her know I was still outside with her.

Izzy leaned forward. "Wait!" she said.

The man paused and looked at her quizzically.

"I—I mean, please," Izzy faltered, "I know that this is thirty-three. Just, well, I'm a bit lost, and I don't know where to find the one I'm looking for."

Finally, the man took a step out of his doorway. "It's that way," he said, pointing down the road.

I tried to squeeze past him, but there wasn't enough space without bumping into him—and completely giving away the fact that there was an invisible person standing outside his office was the last thing I wanted to do.

"Sorry, which one is it exactly?" Izzy asked. "Can you show me the exact one?"

The man sighed, but he took another step away from his door. "It's five doors down. The one that's set back," he said.

I didn't hear Izzy's reply. I was too busy sneaking inside and getting away from the man before he walked into me and the game was up.

A moment later, the door had closed, the man was heading back inside, and our investigation had well and truly begun.

The first thing I thought as I looked in through a glass door from the hallway was that it reminded me a bit of the chemistry lab at school. The second thing I thought was that, actually, it was *nothing* like the chemistry lab at school.

How it was similar to a chemistry lab: It was filled with scientific equipment and desks. A couple of long Formica tables ran along one side of the room, each with a tall black swivel chair tucked in beside it. Above the desks ran a long shelf, packed with jars, bottles, tubes, and boxes, each with a neatly written label. Each desk had a computer and a load of paperwork. The first desk was arranged neatly with a pile of books, a tray of folders, and a desk planner. The other was covered in a heap of notebooks and papers that were arranged in the kind of mess that possibly made sense to the person who owned them but looked like an amateur burglary had taken place to anyone else.

Across the other side of the room there was one long work surface. On it stood a huge microscope, surrounded by various racks with different size test tubes propped up in them. Some of the tubes were empty; others had different sorts of liquid in them. It was hard to tell what the liquids could have been: some were clear, others colored. There was a purple one, a pink one, a deep blue, a yellow, and a green.

So far, a chemistry lab.

How it was different from a chemistry lab: To start with, as the man stepped toward the glass door into the main area, the door slid open with a soft *whshhhhh* noise that sounded a bit like the spaceship doors on *Star Trek* and not at all like the door to our chemistry lab. I quickly stepped through behind him and looked back as the door closed with another *whshhhhh* followed by a soft *clthnnnk*.

My heart did a tiny *clthnnnk* itself as I discovered that I was now hermetically sealed into a lab that I was gradually realizing looked like a cross between a high-tech experimentation center and a chemistry classroom from a hundred years in the future.

Bright lights shone down from the ceiling so fiercely that I felt almost pinned to the floor by them. White walls, white ceiling—everything was spotless and clinical.

Machines beeped and whirred and clicked and buzzed all around me. Just down from the microscope and test tubes was a metal box with orange buttons and red lights blinking above. Next to that sat a bright-blue box with a silver tube running from it up to a white tray on a high shelf. Beyond that, another machine bleeped every thirty seconds. Then there was something that looked like a metal bowl, but it had a digital display on it with numbers that flashed up in pink every few seconds.

There was only one tiny window at the far end of the room: small, high up, and frosted so no one could see in.

What on earth *was* this place?

The man put on a pair of plastic goggles and took up from where we had presumably disturbed him, studying liquids in tubes and scribbling notes.

I tiptoed past him and made my way to the far end of the lab. I tried to read some of the notes.

They were computer printouts adorned with additions handwritten in multiple colors.

Sentences were crossed out and written over. Footnotes with asterisks and hashtags littered the margins. Equations that would have made my math teacher faint were randomly scattered in between barely legible notes.

None of it meant the slightest thing to me — until I noticed a large white plastic box at the back of the desk.

It was full of crystals. Piles of them, lying in groups.

I swallowed. This was definitely him, then — the man who'd bought a heap of crystals from the same shop where Nancy had bought my necklace!

But what did all this mean? What did he want with the crystals? What were all the test tubes for? And what on earth was I to make of his notes?

I kept silent and watched the man work. After a couple of minutes, he left his test tubes and crossed the room to start punching buttons on one of the machines. A moment later, a handheld gadget on the table beeped. He picked it up and read the screen. Still holding it, he moved over to one of the computers. I silently dodged out of his way as he came right past me. Glancing at the screen of the gadget in his hand, he started typing into his computer.

I stood behind him, holding my breath, and watched as he typed. He was muttering to himself, but I couldn't make out what he was saying.

It looked like he was inputting data into a spreadsheet—numbers and words. I peered at the screen, and a moment later, I had to bite my finger to stop myself from yelping out loud.

Among all the gobbledygook, three words had jumped out at me as if they were written in bright-red capitals and underlined three times: ROSE QUARTZ: INVISIBLE?

For a moment, I just stared. My thoughts dried up. My blood froze in my veins. What did this mean? Was he the person who had given me superhuman powers? Was that what this place was about? Injecting weird liquids into crystals to make them do what the rose quartz had done to me? Or had he just discovered the rose quartz's properties like I had?

Either way, something super weird was going on, and if his chart was anything to go by, this man knew a whole lot more about it than I did. I tried to make some kind of sense of his spreadsheet, but other than those three words, the rest was a complicated mass of data that meant about as much to me as it would have had it been in another language.

If it hadn't been essential that I remain silent, I would have kicked myself. Why hadn't I concentrated better on the spreadsheet lessons in school? I might have been able to make *some* sort of sense of it then. If only Izzy were here with me. She'd understand it much better than I could.

I had a thought.

I slipped my hand into my pocket and drew out my phone. Double-checking that it was on silent, I found the camera button and took a shot of the computer screen.

Then I hit the button to open a new text. I typed my message and sent it to Izzy.

"Get me out!"

Chapter 9

"You again!"

The man was standing in the doorway, blocking it completely.

Izzy was outside, a bottle of lemonade in her hand and her bag slung over her shoulder. "I just wanted to let you know that I found number twenty-three, in case you'd been worried."

"Good," the man said. "I wasn't worrying about it, actually, but I'm very happy for you. Now, if that's all . . ."

"Yes, that's all," Izzy said. "And, thank you."

"All right. Well, you're welcome." The man was starting to close the door.

No! Izzy, don't go! I'm still inside!

Izzy turned to leave, but as she moved, she tripped, dropping her bottle on the ground. "Whoops, sorry," she said as lemonade spilled everywhere. The man jumped back. Instantly, I squeezed through the doorway and didn't stop running till I was down the path and halfway up the road.

Izzy caught up with me as I was crouching low behind a hedge, turning myself visible again. "Thanks!" I said. "Come on, let's get out of here."

As we walked, I filled Izzy in on everything I'd seen. At the bus stop, I got my phone out and showed her the picture of the computer screen. "What do you think?"

"I don't get it," Izzy said, squinting at the photo. "What does it all mean? What are those numbers? And why all the other crystals?"

"I don't know," I admitted. "But I figure he must either be experimenting on them all to see which ones make you invisible or doing something to the crystals to make it happen."

"I agree. But even if he is, we still don't know why it only works on you."

I shook my head. "I know. I don't get any of it."

"Maybe we should ask Nancy," Izzy suggested.

"No."

"Why not?"

I thought about her question, and I wasn't sure of the answer. I told myself it was because Nancy probably didn't know anything. Just because she knew this man didn't mean she knew what he was up to with the crystals.

The real truth was more complicated, though. Nancy had been like an aunt to me my whole life. I couldn't *bear* the thought that she might have something to do with all this—that she could be using me as part of some kind of experiment. If that *was* the truth, I wasn't ready to hear it yet. And I wasn't sure how to explain all that to Izzy, either.

"I just don't want to," I said in the end.

Izzy nodded. Maybe she understood without my having to explain.

"I know who we *could* ask," she said after a while.

"Who?"

"Tom."

"Tom? We can't involve him in this! We can't tell *anyone* about it!"

"Come on, Jess, it's Tom. He's the one person we both know we can trust. He wouldn't tell anyone else," Izzy argued. "And I figure we could use

90

a brain like his on the case. We don't even have to tell him about you turning invisible."

I frowned. "Really?"

"Really. Not if you don't want to. We could just show him the spreadsheet and see what he makes of it."

I thought for a moment. Izzy was right. Tom loved solving logic problems even more than Izzy did. If anyone could make sense of this, it was probably him. And she was right that we could trust him, too. "OK. Let's get him on board," I said as the bus rounded the corner.

Izzy already had her phone out.

"What are you doing?"

"Texting him to tell him to meet us at my house. We can send the pic to my computer and blow it up so we can see it better. We'll show it to Tom and ask him what he thinks of the chart. You can be in charge of how much we tell him. OK?"

I nodded at Izzy as we got on the bus. "OK."

Forty-five minutes later, Izzy and I were sitting at her kitchen table with her laptop open, waiting for it to boot up so we could open the picture, when the doorbell rang.

"That must be Tom," I said.

Izzy jumped up to let him in.

"Hey, girls," Tom said with a smile as he came into the kitchen. "What's going on? What's with the weird text?" He sat down at the table and waited for one of us to answer.

I looked at Izzy. She looked at me. And then I said, "Look, you're going to find some of this hard to believe, but as long as you promise to keep it to yourself, I'm going to tell you everything—and all of it's true."

Tom's smile faltered a little. "Sounds ominous," he replied nervously. "Go on, then."

So I did. I told him everything that had happened. Tom listened in silence to the whole thing.

When I'd finished, he stared at me with his mouth open. He glanced briefly at Izzy, then back at me. And then he burst out laughing.

"What's so funny?" Izzy asked.

"This! This—story, or whatever. It's great. I love it. You two crack me up with your crazy stuff."

"Tom, this isn't crazy stuff," I hissed. "Well—I mean, yeah, it is *pretty* crazy. But it's not a story. It's true."

Tom leaned in closer. "You're honestly telling me that you can turn invisible?" he whispered.

"Yes!"

"And that there's some sci-fi lab in the middle of town full of crystals and charts and potions and mad scientists that might be responsible for it? Which, by the way, would actually be the coolest thing in the world, if it *did* exist."

"It *does* exist!" Izzy insisted.

Tom scowled. "Really? I mean, *really*?"

I stood up. "Tom," I said impatiently, "watch." And then I took a deep breath, cleared my mind — and turned myself invisible.

Tom's eyes looked as if they might actually pop out from his face. He turned to Izzy. "She . . . she . . ."

"Yeah," Izzy replied. "She turned invisible. Just like she said."

I made myself visible again and sat down. "Now do you believe us?" I asked.

Tom swallowed and nodded.

Izzy reached for her laptop and clicked on her e-mail. "Now that we've got that settled," she said, "take a look at this. See if you can make any more sense of it than we could."

"OK," he said. His voice was a bit shaky. "I—sorry, Jess. I mean, I didn't think you were actually lying, I just found it a bit hard to believe."

"Don't worry about it," I told him. "So did I at first!"

"But, I mean, how is this even possible?" he went on. "Like, scientifically? Mathematically? Logically?"

"Maybe not everything is logical and mathematical," Izzy countered.

Tom gave her the kind of look most people would give you if you'd suggested that the moon had turned orange and had cows grazing on it.

"*Everything* is mathematical," he insisted. "Even things you can't see, like atoms. Even nature. The tides, the moon, the petals on a flower. All of it is—"

"Look, we can't explain it," I said, waving a hand to stop Tom before he got going on his favorite subject and we ended up straying too far from what we were here to do. "Not yet. That's why you're here. To help us figure it all out."

Tom cleared his throat and leaned toward the laptop. "OK," he said. "Let's have a look at this picture."

The three of us stared at it in silence for a couple of minutes.

Eventually, Tom sat back and shook his head. "I don't know what to make of it," he said. "I mean, obviously, it's a classic database-oriented spreadsheet, but too much of it is using unidentifiable markers. Without being able to quantify the algorithm, it's almost impossible to identify the linear dependence among the variable data to provide a valuable analysis."

I tried to look at Tom in a way that implied I had a clue what he had just said.

"Come again?" Izzy asked.

Tom thought for a moment. "Sorry. I forgot we speak different languages." He slowed down, as if talking to someone who'd only just learned to speak English. "Basically, a lot of this is in code, and until we can crack the code so we understand what all the initials refer to, this chart doesn't give us much to go on. Does that make more sense?"

"I think so. Do you think you could crack it?" I asked.

Tom shook his head. "To be honest, from this picture alone, I doubt it. There just isn't enough information to go on. I can give it a try, but don't hold out too much hope. E-mail it to me and I'll study it at home tonight. I'll let you know if I come up with anything."

Izzy tapped a few keys on the laptop. "OK, done. Thanks, Tom."

I thought for a moment. "All of which leaves us no closer than we were before we found the lab."

Tom looked at me. "You know, there's another way you can find out what's going on here."

"What's that?" I asked.

"You could ask the man."

"The man from the lab?"

"Uh-huh. The scientist, or whatever he is. He's the only person you know who could definitely give you some information."

Izzy nodded slowly. "Tom's got a point— except I can't exactly see him opening up to us after we've already annoyed him."

Izzy was right. She couldn't knock on his door for a third time, and there was no way I was going on my own.

I had another thought. "Wait! Didn't you write down his phone number as well as his address?"

Izzy rifled in her bag and fished out her

notebook. She flipped it open and showed me the page with the man's details on it—address and phone number.

"You're right. We can't go back there," I said. "But we could call him and get him to meet us. He won't know it's us from a phone call."

"Make sure you meet him somewhere neutral. And public," Tom said. "Just to be on the safe side."

"And somewhere he can't slam a door in our faces," Izzy added.

"At the park?" I suggested.

"Perfect," Izzy agreed. "How about the green bench with all the graffiti by the lake?"

"Great," I agreed. "Plus, it's nice and public, just in case he gets seriously annoyed with us. Tomorrow morning?"

Tom frowned. "I've got Math Olympics practice tomorrow at eleven. I won't be free till early afternoon."

Math Olympics is an interschool math competition, and Tom is one of the star members of our team. Most boys Tom's age would probably do something like play soccer in the park on a Sunday, but then, Tom isn't most boys—which is partly why Izzy and I like hanging around with him. He's good company, even if he can be a tad geeky. And at times like this, geeky was no bad thing.

"How about we start without you?" Izzy suggested. "Text us when you're free and we'll let you know where we are."

"Cool. I'll meet you afterward." Tom grinned. "Can't wait. I don't think I'll be able to concentrate on math."

"Wow," Izzy countered. "That would be a first!" Then she passed me the card with the scientist's number on it. "Go ahead."

"Wait. Why me?" I asked.

"I've spoken to him too many times already. He might recognize my voice. There's no way he'll talk to me after I stopped by twice *and* spilled lemonade all over him."

I looked at Tom. He held his hands up in front of him. "Hey, I'm just here as an adviser," he said. "Plus, well, come on. You know me. I clam up and stammer like an idiot with people I don't know. I think this should come from you."

"I suppose you're right." My mouth went dry as I keyed the scientist's number into my phone.

"You can do it," Izzy said.

The line rang four times before an automated

voice kicked in. "I am sorry, but the person you are calling . . ."

I put my hand over the receiver. "Voice mail."

Izzy grimaced. "Leave a message!"

I calmed my breathing while the voice continued, "Please leave your message after the tone."

The line buzzed and went silent. I cleared my throat.

"This is a message for the scientist at the laboratory on Albany Road," I said, throwing a "Help me out!" look at Izzy and Tom.

Izzy smiled encouragingly. Tom gave me a double thumbs-up. "Go on," he whispered. "You're doing great!"

"It's about the crystals," I went on, trying to make my voice sound as confident and authoritative as possible. "And it's about . . ." I cleared my throat again. "It's about invisibility."

I glanced at Izzy and Tom again. They were both nodding vigorously.

"I believe that we may be able to help each other. If you want to know more, come to Smeaton's Park, tomorrow, at one o'clock. We will meet you on the graffiti-covered bench next to the lake. Please do not tell anyone about this call. Thank you."

I ended the call and put my phone down. My heart was hammering so hard it was giving me chest pains.

"Fantastic," Tom said, smiling broadly.

"We're on for one o'clock tomorrow," added Izzy.

"Yeah," I said as I tried to gather my thoughts. The only problem was, they refused to be gathered. They were too busy turning into butterflies and chasing one another around my stomach.

The next day at 12:55, I was standing at the park gates. Izzy arrived a couple of minutes later.

"Sorry I kept you waiting," she said breathlessly. "Mom made me clean my room before coming out."

"I haven't been here long," I said. "Come on, let's get to the meeting point."

We reached the bench by the lake. It was empty.

"I'm going to stay just out of sight," Izzy said. "I don't want the man to recognize me and leave before you've had a chance to talk. But I'll be close by. OK?"

I nodded.

"You ready?" Izzy asked.

"Kind of," I said with a grimace. I sat down on the bench while she wandered off to wait on the other side of a tree next to the lake.

If it hadn't been for the fact that I was so nervous that I thought I might be sick, it could actually have been kind of fun. In a *hey-look-the-world's-gone-crazy-and-you've-suddenly-got-a-superpower-and-are-about-to-meet-up-with-a-mad-scientist-in-the-park* kind of way.

I tried to relax, but then I realized I couldn't let myself. If I calmed my breathing and relaxed my mind too much, I might start accidentally turning invisible! And since I was sitting in the park in broad daylight, about to meet a strange man, that might not be the best thing I could do at that point. So I just sat there with my head down, fighting the urge to be sick and hoping he'd turn up soon.

"Jessica?"

A familiar voice startled me out of my thoughts. I looked up. Nancy! What was she doing here? She couldn't be here! The scientist was due to show up any minute. I had to get rid of her!

"I . . . er, I . . . hi!" I said. Cool as anything. "I can't really talk at the moment. Sorry. Nice to see you, but I'm too busy to chat right now."

Nancy must not have heard me properly—either that or she was terrible at taking a hint. She sat down next to me.

I stared at her, mouth open. "This seat is saved!" I blurted out. What a stupid thing to say. You can't save seats in the park. But what else could I say? Why wasn't she taking the hint?

She reached over and took hold of my hand. "It's good to see you, Jess," she said softly.

"Um. Yeah. You too," I said, trying for a smile, but probably doing that thing with my face that you do when your mom puts on a dress that does *nothing* for her and you tell her how great she looks.

I pried my hand away from her and stood up. I'd have to hide out somewhere and wait for the man to turn up. I'd spot him when he got here and I'd give him some sort of signal. I'd figure something out. "I'm really sorry," I said. "I can't stop. I've got things to do."

Nancy stood up, too. She looked at me, an unreadable expression on her face. "Sit down, Jess," she said.

"I can't!" I said, starting to panic. "See, I'm going to be late . . ."

"Jessica," Nancy said in a tone of voice I'd never heard her use before. "Sit."

I stared at her. Like a good dog, I sat.

I glanced at my watch. Nearly ten past one. He'd probably seen the two of us here and wouldn't come over till I was on my own. I *had* to get rid of Nancy. "I'm waiting for someone," I said feebly.

Nancy took a long, slow breath. Then she turned and looked me straight in the eye. "Jess," she said, "you're waiting for me."

Chapter 10

I spent the next minute or two staring blankly at Nancy with my mouth open. I was glad it wasn't summertime or I'd have swallowed at least half a dozen flies.

"I'm waiting for you?" I managed eventually. "I don't understand." At least, I really, really didn't *want* to understand.

"Of course you don't," Nancy said softly. "That's why I'm here. I've come to explain."

"OK," I said. "Look, can Izzy join us? She's here, too. She came for moral support."

"Of course she can." Nancy looked around us.

"She's, um, she's behind that tree over there," I said, waving Izzy over.

"OK, ready," I said as Izzy joined us and I shifted along the bench to make room for her.

"Sure?" Nancy asked, giving Izzy a quick smile. We both nodded.

Nancy took a breath. "OK. So, some years ago, when I'd just started working as a midwife, one of the doctors at the hospital told me he was starting a research project."

Research. The word made my insides flutter. Research, as in a lab full of books and test tubes and computers and supersonic doors and bright lights and high-tech equipment for experimenting on people like me? I kept quiet and waited for Nancy to continue.

"He'd won a grant from a new government department and asked me to join him. He was trying to find a cure for . . ." Nancy cleared her throat. "Well, for all sorts of illnesses that there was no cure for. Only, it didn't work. Then, when the funding got cut, James gave up. On everything."

"James?"

"Dr. Malone. My colleague. For a long time, we didn't even talk about it." Nancy twirled a thick dreadlock around her fingers. "Just a couple of months ago, he approached me about starting up our research again." She turned to look at us both. Her eyes seemed to have an extra sparkle in them. "James is one of the best doctors I knew. He's done things others wouldn't even attempt; he sees links that everyone else misses. The man is a genius. If he wanted to give it another try, I was in."

"What made him think it would work now if it hadn't worked then?" I asked.

"He didn't know if it would or not, but he wanted to try. It was exactly ten years since . . . well, since everything had fallen apart. Plus, he'd come into some money, which meant he could restart the project without government support. He rented an office space, turned it into a lab, and we started working to catch up with where we'd left off." Nancy paused.

"And?" Izzy prompted.

"And it was hard. When we'd abandoned the project a decade ago, James destroyed virtually everything to do with it. That meant we were starting from scratch. But then we had a breakthrough."

Nancy hesitated and glanced at me. "It was around your birthday," she went on. "I'd been shopping for a present for you. I saw something nice in a shop in town."

"Tiger's Eye?"

Nancy nodded. "There were a few things that I liked. The necklace I gave you and a couple of bracelets. One with an amethyst in it, the other with a moonstone. I couldn't decide which to get, so I bought all three and decided I'd give you one and keep the other two myself."

"Did you know there was anything . . . *special* about the crystals?" I asked, suddenly realizing it was possible that Nancy *still* didn't know what the crystals did. Possible, but unlikely.

"No," she replied. "It was a couple of days after your birthday that everything changed. I'd left the two bracelets in the lab. James was on one side of the room, using the centrifuge in an experiment to separate isotopes so we could analyze the components of our serum."

I stared blankly at Nancy, wondering why she'd suddenly started talking in a foreign language.

Nancy noticed my face. "Basically, he was working on a controlled experiment with lots of delicate items. Meanwhile, I was rushing around doing too many things at once and not concentrating properly on any of them."

"Sounds like an accident waiting to happen," Izzy mused.

"Exactly. James was at a crucial moment. He'd assessed the sedimentation principle with all the different variables, and —"

Nancy stopped as she looked from me to Izzy.

"OK, basically, James had poured the serum into a special kind of bowl, and at that exact moment, I swung around, grabbed my hospital bag from a shelf, and knocked the amethyst bracelet into that bowl."

"Yikes!" I exclaimed.

"Yes. James had spent hours getting to this point in his experiment and he wasn't happy, but then something incredible happened. The bowl began to vibrate—ever so gently—and the serum inside it frothed and fizzed."

I felt the hairs on my arm tingle as Nancy talked.

"And then, the strangest thing of all," she continued, "the bracelet itself came right out of the bowl and hovered above it for a few seconds. A moment later, it fell back down, the serum stopped fizzing, and it was as though nothing had happened."

"Wow!" Izzy blinked at Nancy. "What did you do?"

"To begin with, we stared at the space above the bowl, not speaking. I think we were both afraid to be the first one to say what we'd just seen in case the other one told us we were crazy."

Yup, I knew all about *that* one.

"Once we'd recovered from the shock, we fished out the bracelet and put the other one in the serum. The bowl shook and the serum fizzed again. But this time, when we took the crystal out, it was ice-cold. We didn't know what any of this meant, but we knew that something big was going on."

I suddenly fit a piece of the jigsaw puzzle into place. "And then you took the doctor back to Tiger's Eye, where he bought as many crystals as possible so you could try them all with the serum and see what happened!"

"That's right. He was so excited. It was as if he had a new lease on life. I hadn't seen him like this since . . . well, I hadn't seen him like this for a very long time."

I nibbled on my thumbnail. "Did he buy a rose quartz?"

"It was the first one we tried. I kept thinking about you and the birthday present I'd given you a week earlier. At that point, I had no real reason to think it would have done anything but, even so, I wanted to find out what it *could* do."

"And? What happened when you put that one in the liquid?" I prompted.

Nancy met my eyes. "It turned invisible."

I held her gaze. Could she tell? Did she know

that I could turn invisible, too? Should I ask? Eventually, I said in a quiet voice, "It did the same to me."

Nancy nodded and released a breath that came out in a low whistle. "What happened?" she asked. "How did you find out?"

I filled her in on what had been going on. How the crystal didn't work on Izzy but it worked on me. How I had to clear my mind for it to take effect.

"That's interesting," Nancy mused when I told her this. "It must have something to do with the clarity of the crystal mixing with the purity of the serum."

OK, whatever.

"So, why me?" I asked. "Why does it work on me?"

"That question hasn't been out of my head since I heard your voice mail message at the lab," Nancy said. "We haven't tested it on people, only inanimate objects."

"Why?" Izzy asked.

"It's too powerful, and we don't know enough about it yet. My sense is that the older the person is, the stronger the likelihood of it being dangerous or unpredictable."

"Why do you say that?" Izzy persisted.

Nancy frowned as she thought. "OK, I'll try to keep it simple. The serum we developed is at the heart of all this. We have deduced that if the serum interacts with certain crystals and stones, it produces astounding results."

"I'm with you so far," Izzy confirmed.

"Without going into the complexities, we think certain conditions need to be met in order for the serum to work on people," Nancy went on. "These have to do with cell multiplication, brain development, and method of ingestion."

"OK, you're starting to lose me now," I said.

Nancy smiled. "You don't need to understand all the scientific ins and outs."

"You still haven't explained why it works on Jess and no one else," Izzy reminded her.

"Well, I can't say for sure, but I've got a theory."

We waited for her to continue.

"One day, early on in our research, a couple of things happened that we didn't think much of at the time, but which I've been looking at differently over the last couple of weeks."

I raised my eyebrows. "Like?"

"Like what happened on a certain day just

over thirteen years ago. I was running late for my shift. James was carrying a rack of tubes full of the latest version of our serum. The phone rang. I ran to answer it—and we collided. The tubes went everywhere."

"You broke all the test tubes?"

"Yup. I got absolutely covered in the serum, literally from head to toe. I cleaned myself up and left James to deal with the rest of it. I was already late and I had three patients in labor who needed me."

I swallowed. "Thirteen years ago. Three patients in labor," I said calmly. "And my mom was one of them."

Nancy turned and looked me in the eye. "Yes. All three gave birth on that shift." She allowed herself a small smile. "You were the first."

I stared at Nancy for a while, trying to figure out exactly what she was telling me. "Are you saying that this serum somehow got into me when I was born?" I asked eventually.

Nancy nodded. "Obviously, I had no idea at the time. I thought I'd gotten rid of every bit of the serum. I would never knowingly expose a brand-new baby to any form of experimental liquid."

Izzy frowned. "So why did you suspect something had happened to Jess?"

"At the end of my shift, when I took my scrubs off to wash them, I noticed a tiny bit of the serum on the inside of my sleeve. I must have missed it. I had a brief panic, but once I knew all three babies were all right, I stopped worrying about it. I assumed that it hadn't touched them and, anyway, at that point the serum still hadn't achieved anything as far as we knew, so I didn't give it another thought."

"Till now," I said.

"Exactly. A couple of weeks ago, when we discovered that the serum reacts with crystals, I started worrying again. I remembered your birth, thought about the necklace I'd just given you. I was in quite a state. I even tried to find out from your mom if anything unusual had happened to you."

"That night," I said. "I heard you."

"You heard us? I thought you were upstairs."

I shook my head and looked down, felt my cheeks burn. "I was invisible."

Nancy laughed softly. "I didn't realize you'd found out anything till I heard your message—I didn't know if it had had any effect on you. I still

113

had no real reason to think it would have. It's never worked on anyone else."

"Really? No one at all?"

Nancy's eyes darkened and she turned away. "Well, there was one time . . ." She held up a hand as if to brush away the rest of her sentence. "But, look, that was completely different, and it was soon after that that we stopped work on the serum—until James started it up again. As far as I know, the serum has never had this effect on anyone else."

"How come it didn't work on you, if you got it all over yourself, but it *did* work on me?"

Nancy shrugged. "I can't be sure, but I think that it must be because you were a baby, not a fully grown adult, when you were exposed to the serum. A brand-new baby's cells are multiplying and developing much more quickly than an adult's, making them more receptive."

"So it's always been there? I've had this thing in me all my life?" I asked.

"Probably."

"Wow!"

"You've just never known it until you wore a crystal that acted with it to produce an effect. Plus—and this is where it gets a little complicated . . ." Nancy glanced at me. I gave her a quick nod to carry on.

"Part of my current theory is that the serum works best when it interacts with specific changes in human physiology."

"OK . . ." Izzy and I said together.

"So it only took hold of you as a baby because of the rate at which your cells were multiplying. But since then it has probably been lying dormant until another important developmental stage—the development of your frontal lobe."

"Frontal what?" Izzy asked.

"It's part of your brain—the part that interacts with the serum to activate its capacity to interface with the crystals. Around your age, the frontal lobe goes through a massive growth spurt. Things are changing in your brain at a really accelerated pace. I think that's what triggered the serum into acting and why it's only now that it has become effective."

"So what if Jess had come into contact with a crystal when she was younger?" Izzy asked.

Nancy shook her head. "It almost certainly wouldn't have done anything."

I let out a breath. "Wow," I said again. What else *could* I say?

Nancy pulled on one of her dreadlocks that had come loose and tucked it back under her hairband. "I'd never forgive myself if anything happened to you because of this. If anyone finds out and you get into any kind of bad situation . . . Jess, you know I would never have given you the necklace if I'd had any idea . . ."

"Of course I do," I said. "But you would never have gotten this far with your research if you *hadn't* bought me the necklace."

"I know. It's all just feeling a little complicated. I want you to know I would never have knowingly put you in this position."

I nodded. "I know that. What else is complicated?"

"Well, James and I could get into massive trouble for continuing to work on this. If it gets out that we've continued working on research that the government killed over a decade ago, it won't look good for either of us."

"What would happen?"

"We'd both lose our jobs, that's for sure. Probably our licenses to practice at all." She glanced at our faces. "But, look, you don't need to worry about that. It's my problem. You've got enough to deal with."

"Are you going to tell the doctor about Jess?" Izzy asked.

Nancy shook her head. "He doesn't need anything else to worry about. He's the world's biggest stress-head at the best of times, and the more he has on his mind, the more it interferes with things."

"Interferes? What do you mean?" I asked.

"Oh, you know. Silly things. Like, for the last couple of weeks, he's been so wrapped up in his research that he's gotten quite distracted and absentminded and then he does stupid things— such as forgetting to file documentation or putting vials away in the wrong places. He leaves things out. Some crystals have gone missing, and I'm having to clean up after him just to make sure we keep track of everything we're doing—and so we can be certain the wrong people don't get wind of these new developments."

I was about to ask who exactly these "wrong people" were when Nancy waved her hand dismissively again. "Anyway," she said, "I've done more than enough talking." She stood up.

"Is that it?" I asked. "Are you leaving?"

"Not leaving, no. But you must be tired of these long-winded explanations. I thought you might like some action instead."

"Action?" Izzy asked as we both got up from the bench, too. "What kind of action?"

Nancy smiled. "You'll see," she said. "We need to go somewhere private, though. What I want to show you both is pretty astounding—and top secret!"

"How about the Meadows?" I suggested. That's what we called the fields and woodland that lay between the park and the river.

"Perfect," Nancy said. "Are you ready?"

I glanced at Izzy. Her eyes were wide as she pushed her glasses up her nose. "Ready for what, exactly?" she asked.

Nancy had already started walking away. "Follow me," she said. "You'll find out when we get there."

Chapter 11

Nancy led us to a small clearing in the Meadows. Around us, grass rose as high as our waists. "Help me pat it down," she said, stamping her feet on the grass to create a flattened space.

Once she'd decided we had enough room, she bent low and opened her bag. I went over to look as she pulled things out of it: a metal bowl on a wire stand, a piece of cloth with about ten different crystals wrapped in it, and a thin glass bottle filled with clear liquid.

"You just happen to carry these things around with you?" I asked.

Nancy laughed. "No. I just happened to think you might want to see some of this." She looked from Izzy to me. "Ready to get started?"

"We're ready," I said.

"Good." Nancy bent down and set to work. She picked up one of the crystals. It was a small bunch-like shape in deep green. It looked like a mini broccoli. "This is called malachite," she said. She opened the bottle and poured some clear liquid into the bowl. "I need to use this sparingly," she said. "We don't have much left. But I've got enough to put on a good show for you."

Then she dropped the malachite into the bowl. "Watch," she told us.

Nothing happened for a moment. Then the liquid began to fizz gently, bubbling and clouding over. The malachite bounced around in the bowl as the bubbles formed.

"Look!" Izzy said, gasping as she pointed at the bowl. The crystal was getting bigger. Within half a minute, it had grown to at least three times its original size.

"It'll crack the bowl!" I said.

"It's OK. It doesn't get bigger than this," Nancy replied. We watched as the bubbles gradually subsided and the liquid calmed down. Then Nancy reached in and pulled out the malachite. She handed it to Izzy. It was nearly as big as her hand.

"That's amazing," Izzy said, turning to me. "Do you want to hold it?"

I reached out for the stone, but Nancy put a hand on my arm to stop me. "Wait!" she said.

"What's up?"

"We've done some tests, so I'm sure there's nothing to worry about, but I want to explain something about our results before you touch it, OK?"

"OK," I agreed.

"Each of the crystals is unique, and they all do a completely different thing. Take this one, for example. We had a necklace with a malachite pendant on it. When we put it in the serum, the whole necklace grew—not just the crystal."

"Like the whole of me turns invisible," I said, "and not just the crystal?"

"Right. So we know that if the crystal is physically attached to something when it interacts with the serum, it transfers its powers to the attached object."

"Or person," Izzy added.

"Or person," Nancy agreed. "We've also found that once an object has been given a power from one crystal, it will never gain the power of another one."

"So you mean that now that Jess has turned invisible because of the rose quartz, she won't pick up any other powers even if she touches another crystal?"

"Exactly."

"So it's safe for me to touch the malachite?" I asked.

"According to our tests, yes. And there's no reason to think it will be any different for you. But, look, let's try with a different one, just to be on the safe side. One that *definitely* won't make you grow to three times your size!"

Nancy held her hand out and Izzy passed the giant broccoli back to her. "It'll go back to its original size in a little while," Nancy said, placing it back on the cloth and picking up another stone. It was light purple and shaped like a mini tower with a tiny hole in the top. "Here, let's try this one," she said.

"What is it?" I asked.

"Amethyst."

Izzy and I leaned in to study the crystal. The bottom half was a deeper purple than the top and looked as though it had been crushed and condensed. The top half was so light it was see-through. As the sun caught it, it glinted and sparkled.

"Amethyst was the one that flew when you put it in the serum," Izzy said.

"Good memory," Nancy confirmed. "OK, watch."

She went through the process again. The crystal bounced and shook inside the serum. A few moments later, it rose out of the bowl, hovering above it. It climbed as high as our heads. After a few minutes, it gradually came back down and Nancy caught it.

Izzy stared, openmouthed, at the amethyst. "It's beautiful," she breathed.

I stared at it, too. Nancy saw me looking and held it out to me. "You want to try touching it?" she asked.

Accidentally being able to fly was definitely less of a problem than accidentally growing to three times my size. I reached out for the crystal. Nancy and Izzy studied me as I turned it over in my hands.

Nothing happened. I closed my eyes and cleared my mind, just to double-check. Still nothing. Actually, not quite nothing. I could feel myself starting to turn invisible, but my feet were still firmly on the ground. I opened my eyes before Nancy could notice my fingers starting to disappear.

"You're fine," she said. "I knew you would be."

"Too bad," Izzy said. "Being able to fly would be *amazing*!"

I passed her the crystal. "You want to hold it?"

Izzy took the amethyst from me and closed her fingers around it. "If I could have any superpower in the world, it would be the ability to fly," she said dreamily.

"You can keep it if you like," Nancy said.

"Really?"

"You know it won't have any effect on you, though, don't you?"

Izzy smiled. "Yeah, I know, but I can always imagine." She put the crystal in her coat pocket and zipped it shut. "Thank you," she said.

"Here, let me show you some others."

Nancy picked up what looked like a jet-black pebble with a few faint lines running across its middle.

Izzy peered at the stone. "What's that?"

"Onyx." Nancy held it out. "Here. Feel it."

Izzy took the stone from Nancy, weighed it in her hands for a moment, then held it out to me.

I took the onyx from Izzy. "It's like a stone," I said. "Hard. Cold. Smooth."

Nancy took the onyx back and dropped it into the serum. "OK, watch this."

Just as it had with the malachite, the liquid soon began to bubble gently. I kept my eyes on the onyx as it spun around in the bowl. For a moment, nothing happened. Then it began to change. It didn't look like a stone anymore; it had stretched and elongated. Nancy reached in and picked it out of the bowl. She handed it to me.

The onyx felt like rubber. It flopped over my fingers. I pulled it and it stretched as thin as paper and as long as my arm. Then I scrunched it up and folded it into a ball. I threw it to Izzy. "Catch."

She missed it and the onyx flew past her. It hit a rock on the ground and bounced up in the air at an odd angle. As Izzy ran to catch it, I turned to Nancy.

"I don't get it," I said. "Why are these things happening? What's it all about?"

"We don't get it, either," Nancy said. "We've worked so hard on these formulas, trying to find a breakthrough in cures for rare illnesses. We were never looking for this. To be honest, it's turned our lives upside down."

"Yeah, you and me both," I said.

Izzy was back with the bouncy onyx and a huge smile. "This is *incredible*!" she said, eyeing the other crystals on the cloth.

Nancy saw her looking. "Come on," she said. "I'll show you a few more."

We huddled around and watched while Nancy gave us a demonstration of more crystals and their superpowers: a bright-green piece of jade that split itself in two; a silver pebble called snowflake obsidian that disappeared from the bowl and reappeared ten feet away, lying on the ground; a piece of topaz that turned to ice.

"Wow, you're lucky you bought Jess a rose quartz," Izzy said. "What if it had been one of these? She could have ended up as an ice statue or something!"

I glared at Izzy.

"I'm sorry I got you into all this," Nancy said softly. "I really am."

"It's OK," I said. "It's cool. OK, it's a bit weird, but it's amazing, too. I get to be a kind of super-human superfreak."

Nancy grimaced. "It's too bad your super-powers can't tell me more about what's going on at the lab."

"You mean about the doctor losing things?" Izzy asked.

Nancy nodded, then shrugged. "I'm sure it's

126

just James being careless. I don't even want to think about the other option."

"Which is what?" I asked.

Nancy turned away. "That someone's been breaking in," she said under her breath. Then she gave us a quick smile. "I'm sure I'm wrong, though. The only way in is a coded keypad, and it hasn't shown any sign of being tampered with. James has got his eye on some very high-tech security — motion sensors and all that — but outfitting the lab with the latest scientific equipment used up James's windfall, so we haven't installed it yet."

"But you think someone *might* be getting in?" I asked.

"I don't know. I'm probably worrying over nothing. I've already told you that James can be absentminded — I'm sure that's all it is. It's just — I like to know exactly where things are and what's going on."

"And you don't," Izzy said.

"No. I've been making charts of all the crystals we've tested and the results we've gained, and I'm sure some of them have gone missing. But it's probably just James doing something with them and forgetting to tell me."

"Why don't you ask him?" Izzy suggested.

Nancy laughed. "You don't know James," she said. "He's so twitchy; the slightest thing could tip him over the edge, and I don't want anything to upset him. Not now that we're finally on the verge of something so exciting—and potentially dangerous."

"Dangerous?" I broke in.

Nancy paused. Her eyes narrowed as she thought. Then she nodded to herself. "I'll show you. Stand back."

We moved back and watched as Nancy picked up a crystal with a pair of tongs. It was an oblong shape and a shimmering amber color. Bright, almost gold, in fact.

"What's that called?" I asked.

"Tiger's eye," Nancy replied without looking up. Now that I looked at it, it actually looked just like the bright amber eye of a tiger. It was the stone the shop was named after.

Nancy dropped the stone carefully into the serum. Just as with all the others, the liquid bubbled and frothed.

"Keep back, now," Nancy warned. She carefully reached into the bowl and lifted the stone out with the tongs. As soon as it was out of the bowl, she threw the stone away from us.

"What are you—?" Izzy began.

"Count to ten," Nancy said, "and watch."

About ten seconds later, I was about to ask what we were supposed to be watching, when—BOOM!—the ground where the stone had landed erupted in a small explosion.

"What the . . . ?" I stared at the smoke rising from the ground.

Nancy waved us over to check it out. We followed her to the spot and watched, openmouthed, as she reached down into a small crater in the burned ground to pick up the stone.

Izzy was staring at me with watery eyes. "What if this had been the one you'd given Jess?" she asked. "Would she have blown herself up?"

"You think I haven't been kept awake at night by precisely that question?" Nancy replied. She handed the stone to Izzy. "Check it out."

I looked over Izzy's shoulder. "It's completely unharmed," I said.

"Exactly. My guess is that you wouldn't have blown *yourself* up—but you might have done some serious damage to things around you."

"Which is why you're so terrified of something like this ending up in the wrong hands," I said.

"Correct." Nancy frowned. "But I can't try to

find out if anyone's been breaking in without set-ting off alarm bells for James — and that's the last thing I want to do. I just have to hope I'm worry-ing about nothing."

"Yeah," I said. But I was thinking, *What if you're not?*

It was only later on, after Nancy had left us and Izzy and I were ambling back through the park, that I decided to share the thoughts that were on my mind. Nancy would never approve so I couldn't tell her — but I was positive Izzy would help me fig-ure it out.

"So, you know how Nancy's worried about what's going on at the lab but doesn't want to bring it up with the doctor?" I began.

"Uh-huh," Izzy said.

"Well. We can help her. We can find out what's going on."

"We can?"

I nodded. Then I glanced around to make sure there was no one around who might overhear our conversation.

The coast was clear. "Listen up," I said. "I've got an idea."

Izzy looked around, too. Then she leaned in to listen. "What's your plan?"

"A stakeout."

"A stakeout?"

"Yep. We hang around the lab out of sight and see if anyone goes in. If they do, I follow them invisibly and see who they are and what they're up to. It's perfect!"

Izzy frowned. "Well, yeah. Apart from one thing."

"What?"

"It might be dangerous."

"How can it be dangerous? No one will see us. We'll keep hidden; they won't know we have anything to do with the lab. And if someone *does* come and I *do* follow them in, I'll be invisible!"

Izzy chewed on a fingernail. "You sure we shouldn't check with Nancy first?"

"Nancy'll just get all nervous and probably say no. And you heard what she said. She's worried. How cool would it be if we do this a couple of times, check there's no one breaking in, and then we can set her mind at rest?"

Izzy took off her glasses and wiped the lenses while she thought. Then she put them back on and nodded. "OK," she said. "Let's do it tomorrow."

Chapter 12

We were just leaving the park when Tom appeared at the gates. He was out of breath, as if he'd been running.

"Good—you're still here!" he exclaimed, falling into stride with us as we walked down the road. "Well? What happened? I want every detail. Even the ones you don't think are important! Tell me everything!"

So we did. Between us, as we walked down the road, heading vaguely into town, Izzy and I relayed everything Nancy had told us—and shown us.

When we'd finished, Tom stopped walking.

I stopped and turned toward him. He was staring at me. His face had lost some of its color. His mouth hung open.

"What?" Izzy asked.

Tom shook his head. "Don't you see? Don't you realize what you've just told me?"

"Er . . . yes. What about it? Is it something to do with Nancy?" Izzy asked.

"No. It's something to do with *me*." Tom looked at me. "To do with *us*."

"Us?" I echoed. "You and me?"

Tom rolled his eyes. "Jess! Three babies born on the same day. In the same ward . . ."

I clapped a hand over my mouth as I suddenly realized what Tom was saying. How could I have missed it?

"You," I said simply. "Of course."

"You were one of the other babies!" Izzy squealed, catching on to my thinking. "That means you might have superpowers, too!"

Tom stared at Izzy as though she'd just said that he'd been born on Mars and his parents were aliens—although, to be fair, Tom was probably the one person in the world who would have thought that sounded like fun. And I guess what she actually *had* said wasn't much less bizarre.

"I can't take this in," he said quietly. He looked down at his feet. "I'm not sure I want something like this."

"Something like what?" I asked.

"I have a hard enough time because I happen to enjoy math and science." He shook his head. "You think I want to be even *more* different?"

I reached out to touch his hand. "Tom, it's OK. It's fun. It's different in a *good* way!"

He shrugged me off. "Sorry, girls." He waved his hands in an "I'm done" kind of gesture and started to walk away. "I just can't handle it. I'm out."

"Tom!" Izzy called down the road to him.

He stopped and turned back to us. "I won't tell anyone," he said. "And it doesn't change anything about our friendship. I'm just—I think I'm maybe just in shock right now. I need some time to myself, OK?"

And then, before we had a chance to reply, he turned on his heel and paced off down the road.

"Should we go after him?" Izzy asked.

I wanted to, but I knew what Tom was going through. I'd been through the same panic and disbelief myself. I'd dealt with it by confiding in Izzy and figuring it out with her. Tom had a different way of handling things. I knew that. And so did Izzy. Tom dealt with worries in the same way he dealt with everything—in his brain, on his own, logically.

"He just needs some space to think things over.

Let's leave him for now. He'll be all right in a couple of days, I'm sure," I said, hoping it was true.

Izzy nodded. We walked in silence, each thinking our own thoughts.

Izzy was the first to speak. When she did, it turned out her thoughts were on the same lines as mine.

"You know it's not just Tom, don't you?" she said.

"Yeah," I replied.

"We just need to find out who the third baby was, and then—"

"No, we don't," I interrupted. Somewhere between Tom reminding me of Nancy's words and Izzy breaking the silence, I'd already realized who the third person was. I wished I hadn't. If you had asked me to compile a list of people I'd rather not be wrapped up in this adventure with, she'd have been somewhere near the top. But I couldn't avoid the truth.

I'd seen her celebrating on the same day as me. I'd overheard her telling her friends how her daddy had bought her a pony for her twelfth birthday. I'd listened to the girls in my grade screeching with delight about her thirteenth birthday party. On the thirtieth of March.

Izzy looked at me quizzically. "You already know?"

I grimaced. "It's Heather."

Izzy looked blank for a moment. Then she registered what I'd said. "Heather Berry? Most-popular-girl-in-our-class? *That* Heather?"

I nodded. "I suppose there might be someone else in town with the same birthday, but my money's on her."

In fact, the more I thought about it, the more convinced I was. I thought back over the last few times I'd seen her—how she'd seemed different. Like that time outside the bathroom.

Then I remembered something else—her new ring!

Was it possible that she'd not only been affected by the serum like me, but that she also had a power like mine and already knew about it? If so, had she guessed that *I* had a superpower, too?

There was only one way to find out.

"Izzy," I said. "We have to speak to Heather."

"Yeah. Only trouble is, how do we do it without sounding insane—or scaring her off like we just did with Tom?"

I thought about it for a second. Then it came to me. "I've got another idea! A stakeout!"

"Yeah, we've already agreed on—"

"No. A *double* stakeout. We do the lab tomorrow evening, but during the day . . ."

"A stakeout of Heather!"

"Exactly. We don't let her know what we're doing. We make it casual. Check out what she's up to, see if there's anything different about her. Be subtle and cool."

"Hmm, subtle and cool. Not exactly our trademark qualities," Izzy pointed out.

"Yeah. Well, you know. We'll do our best."

"And if subtle and cool doesn't work, we could always just come out with it and ask her."

I frowned. "Yeah. Maybe. As long as we can think of a way to say it without ending up at the school counselor's office with a note saying we've lost our marbles."

"Sounds like a plan," Izzy agreed.

And for the first time in roughly . . . well, forever, I realized I was actually looking forward to Monday morning at school.

My first stakeout opportunity was second period—French. Izzy is in honors French. She's in honors everything, actually. I hate French and always have. It's the accent you have to put on when you speak it—I just can't do it. I feel silly trying. I barely made it into French 2.

French must be the one chink in Heather's perfect armor, because she's in the same class.

Before Izzy and I headed separate ways at the end of the hall, Izzy shook my hand, like a general sending his most trusted soldier off to war. "Good luck," she said solemnly. "Or should I say, *bonne chance?*"

"Same to you. See if you can catch up with Tom, check that he's OK."

"Will do," Izzy agreed, and she went into her classroom.

I'd decided my strategy was going to be to start a conversation with Heather and see how she acted with me. I figured I should be able to sense whether there was something different about her.

The problem was, I hadn't quite decided how to actually start the conversation. You can't exactly walk up to someone with whom you've only ever traded dirty looks—apart from in French, when you are forced to talk to each other—and say, "Hi there, I know we've never really spoken, other than to say *'Bonjour, je m'appelle Jessica. Comment vous appelez-vous?'* in a very bad French accent, but I've recently found out that I've got a magical superpower and, hey, guess what! I think you might, too—even if you don't know it yet—so I thought maybe we should try being friends!"

And I was pretty sure that wouldn't be classified as secretly staking her out, either. I'd have to figure it out as I went along.

I walked through the door just before Ms. Hadley got there. I glanced around the room and there was just one seat left—next to Heather! Normally the worst seat I could have landed myself with; today it was ideal.

I slid in next to her and gave her a big smile. She glared at me, then looked away.

This wasn't going to be easy.

A moment later, Ms. Hadley closed the door behind her and looked around the class. Her eyes zoned in on me. "Jessica, were you late?" she asked.

"Um. I don't think so. I was here before you," I said, with a cheeky smile, hoping she'd find me funny and cute.

"Détention," she said. In French.

I sighed as Ms. Hadley told us to get our books out. Then I nearly fell off my chair as Heather nudged me.

"Whoa. That was harsh," she whispered.

"Thanks," I said with a grimace. OK, so it wasn't exactly "Hey, now that we've exchanged five words, let's be BFFs," but it was a start.

I spent the rest of the class with two aims. Aim one: avoid getting into any more trouble with the teacher. I achieved this, as she called me over at the end of class and said she'd decided to let me off the detention since I'd contributed so well, and could I please try to keep that up in the future.

Aim two: smile at Heather as many times as possible so that by the end of a forty-minute class she'd forget our year and a half of animosity and not walk off if I tried to start a conversation with her.

It was during one of these smile attempts that I noticed her hand. She was wearing that sparkly ring again. I was sure I'd never seen her wearing it before last Thursday. Admittedly, I didn't look too closely at her as a rule, but it was bright yellow and shiny and definitely looked new. Might she have gotten it as a birthday present? Was it possible that my suspicion was right—that Heather had already discovered that she had a superpower?

At one point, she caught me staring and I glanced away, but not before noticing that her cheeks had flushed a little and that she quickly put her hand in her pocket.

A bolt of excitement surged through me. I was right! I was sure of it. Well, not *sure*—it was just a feeling, but a strong one. By the end of class, I was too impatient to spend the next few days secretly staking her out. If Heather was like me, I had to know. Now.

She was in front of me as we filed out of the classroom. Once we were in the hall, I seized the moment before my brain seized my courage.

"Hey," I said in my best *now-that-we've-bonded-in-French-class-I'm-sure-you-regard-me-as-one-of-your-best-friends* voice.

Heather turned around.

"Nice ring," I said, pointing at her finger.

Her face clouded over for a second. The way it might have if I'd said, "Hey, you're looking a bit drab today. You almost look as plain as the rest of us."

She recovered quickly, though, and gave me a tiny smile. "Thanks, it's citrine," she said, holding out her hand and looking at the ring. "It was a birthday present."

"Me too!" I burst out. "I mean, I got something for my birthday, too!"

Duh! Most people do get presents on their birthday! Heather was giving me an *OK-I'm-going-to-walk-slowly-away-from-the-crazy-person-now* kind of look. I had to rescue this.

I reached under my shirt. "I mean, I got jewelry. A necklace. On my birthday. Same day as yours." Smooth, Jess, smooth.

I watched Heather's face for a reaction. I didn't see one. Had I been wrong after all?

"Oh. Right," Heather said. "The thirtieth of March?"

"Yep. Same day. Imagine that, huh?"

"I don't . . . I mean, I didn't realize it was your birthday, too."

Obviously not, as you're always too wrapped up in your own celebrations to notice anyone else around you, I would normally have replied. Instead, I smiled and said, "Don't worry about it. Anyway, belated happy birthday—and thanks for being nice to me in French."

Heather gave me the kind of look you might give to a stalker you didn't want to encourage but didn't want to offend, either, because you're a nice person. *Was* she actually a nice person and I'd never realized? "You're welcome," she said with what looked suspiciously like a shy smile.

Heather, shy? Nah, it was much more likely to be a sneer. She'd probably tell her friends all about the stupid conversation with the pathetic loser — aka me — as soon as she saw them.

But there was something about the way she smiled that spurred me on. Before I could stop myself, I gathered all my nerve and a bunch of words charged out of my mouth without checking with my brain first.

"Look. Um. If you're not busy tomorrow at lunchtime, do you want to do something with me?"

"Do something with you?" Heather asked in a voice that was so full of shock I wondered for a second if I had actually asked her if she'd like to rappel off the Eiffel Tower on the back of an elephant.

"I . . . yeah, OK, sorry." How on earth could I have thought Heather would want to spend time with me?

"I have volleyball Tuesdays at lunch," she said.

In other words, *Leave me alone, loser.*

"Yeah. Of course," I said. And then, I don't know what made me do it — probably the thought that this might be my only chance — but I found myself still talking. "Look," I went on. "If anything kind of . . . happens, or if anything has already happened, maybe something weird, that makes you wonder if we've got more in common than you thought . . . and you want to, kind of, you know, hang out, how about Wednesday, then? No pressure. I'll be in the art room at lunchtime. Maybe see you there."

For a moment, Heather almost looked scared—as if I'd just told her she'd been walking around with her skirt tucked into her underwear all day. Then she kind of shook her head and gave me her professional class-president smile. "OK, maybe," she said, "if I'm not busy. But thanks either way," she added, with one final *thank-you-please-leave-me-alone-now-you-weirdo* look.

"Anyway, got to go," I said, and before I could dig myself into a bigger hole, I turned and left her there. The last thing I needed was to be late for my next class and get into trouble yet again.

Chapter 13

I filled Izzy in at lunchtime. We agreed that, since I'd as good as followed Heather around with a sign saying, I'M A WEIRDO. PLEASE BE MY FRIEND, and since we'd disturbed Tom so much that he'd avoided us all morning, we'd probably done everything we could, for the time being.

"I'll talk to Tom in physics," Izzy suggested. "See if he's gotten over it yet."

"Why don't you tell him about Heather? See if he'll join us on Wednesday, too?"

"Good idea. Plus, that gives him another couple of days to get his head around it all."

"Sounds like a plan," I agreed.

It also gave *us* two days to figure out what in the world we were going to say, on the off chance that either of them actually turned up.

And, in the meantime, there was this evening to worry about—the real stakeout.

On Monday evening, I discovered something that I imagine is one of the biggest secrets in the world of undercover policing. A stakeout is not actually all that much fun. It is certainly neither cool nor glamorous, and is possibly the most boring way you could spend a couple of hours.

My back was aching from crouching behind a hedge, my neck was hurting from craning to look down the road, and I was getting cold. Plus, it was a little creepy. It was starting to get dark, and coming up with a plan that involved two girls hiding behind a bush on a quiet street at night suddenly didn't feel like our cleverest moment ever.

Then Izzy grabbed me.

"Jess!" she hissed. She was pointing through a gap in the hedge toward the lab. "Look!"

I peered through the hedge and saw what she was pointing at. Someone was going into the lab! Nancy was right—they *did* have a burglar!

Izzy shoved me. "You need to go. Quickly!"

Suddenly the little-creepy thing became a totally-flipping-crazy-and-terrifying thing instead.

"Wait—what if this person's legitimate? What if it's the doctor?" I pointed out.

"Oh. I hadn't thought of that." Izzy thought for a moment. "Look, if it is someone who's supposed to be there, then it won't do any harm to check, and if it isn't, then we'll have caught the burglar. Win-win!"

"But what if they see me?"

"They won't! You'll be invisible! Go on, quick. They're fiddling with the keypad already. You can follow them in."

There was no time to spare, so rather than hang around panicking and fretting and putting it off—which was what I suddenly realized I mostly wanted to do—I closed my eyes, emptied my mind so I could turn invisible, and stood up.

"Wish me luck," I whispered.

Izzy reached out to touch my arm. She missed it—as I was already invisible and had started moving away. "Good luck. You'll be fine. I'll be right here," she told me.

"OK. You be careful, too," I said. And then I hurried away from the hedge, crossed the road, and crept up behind the person heading into the lab.

I sneaked through the front door and followed through the sci-fi door into the lab. It was only when the figure turned and pulled down his hood that I saw his face for the first time.

I nearly gasped out loud. I knew him!

It was a boy from my school. From my year! He was in the other class, so I didn't know him well. In fact, I'd never spoken to him, but I'd seen him around — Max Something-or-Other.

What on earth was *he* doing here?

I know that, scientifically speaking, it almost certainly isn't possible, but I could swear I didn't breathe for the next thirty minutes. Didn't breathe, didn't think, didn't move. Didn't do anything except watch Max wandering around in the lab.

I didn't know much about him. To be honest, the only reason I'd noticed him at all was that he was kind of a big-mouth. One of those boys who seem to think it's a weakness to smile or be nice to anyone and who always make sure their stupidest comments are said loud enough for everyone to hear.

Not a bully, exactly, just not pleasant, and I'd heard him get into arguments with a few of the other boys after school. I couldn't tell you what they argued about. I'd never hung around long enough to find out, but I'd seen enough to know that this boy wasn't someone I wanted as my best friend. And if he was as unpleasant as he seemed, the thought of him finding out about my secret was not on my list of top things I would love to happen next.

Which was why I held my breath for approximately half an hour, crouched down below a stool—even though I was invisible—and prayed he would leave soon.

Unfortunately, he didn't. He kept wandering around the lab as if he had all the time in the world. He didn't seem to be looking for anything in particular. Every now and then, he'd lean over a table, study something on it, put the occasional thing in his pocket, and move on.

From my hiding place, I couldn't see exactly what he was picking up. I was fairly sure he'd taken a few crystals, as they were all over the place. But what did a boy like him want with rubies and moonstones?

At one point he went to the far wall and opened a cupboard. There were loads of tiny bottles on a shelf inside. They looked like those perfume samples Mom sometimes gets in magazines. Max reached into his pocket and pulled out an identical bottle. He looked at it for a second, his hand hovering in front of the cupboard as if he were about to put it in, then changed his mind and put the bottle back in his pocket.

Eventually, Max seemed to have had enough and headed out into the hall. I silently crept across the lab behind him.

He opened the front door, then left it open as he did his coat up. Time to make a run for it. I shuffled toward him. Was there enough space to get past without touching him? I pondered for a moment, then decided I didn't have any option. I squeezed through the space between Max and the door. Two seconds later, I was out of there!

I was halfway down the path when I heard him.

"Hey, is someone there?" he called.

I froze on the spot. I looked down at myself. Invisible. Totally. He couldn't see me.

I didn't wait any longer. As silently as I could, I crept to the bushes, hissed at Izzy to follow, and ran all the way to the bus stop.

❋

The next day at school, I could hardly believe who I bumped into on the way into assembly. And I mean actually, literally, bumped into—I bashed my face on the back of his shoulder while I was walking along talking to Izzy and not looking where I was going.

Max turned to scowl at me. I stopped breathing, gaped openmouthed at him, and waited for him to recognize me.

"What are you staring at?" he asked in his normal rude way.

Phew! He didn't recognize me. Well, of *course* he didn't recognize me. He hadn't seen me. I'd been invisible!

I'd told Izzy everything when we'd gotten back to her house the night before, and she could see that I'd been thrown by bumping into him.

"She doesn't know," Izzy said. "It hasn't got a label on it." And with that, she grabbed my arm and pulled me in the opposite direction.

I risked a glance in Max's direction before Izzy pulled me away. He had a strange expression on his face. Our eyes met, and for a millisecond, I thought I saw something different in them. Something I'd never seen before. A kind of recognition. What was he seeing? What did *I* recognize?

Izzy whispered to me as we walked down the corridor, "I still don't see what he would want with a bunch of crystals."

"I know," I said. "It doesn't make any sense, does it?" Just like it didn't make any sense that I'd felt a strange kind of connection when our eyes had met. I didn't tell Izzy that, though. She'd only tease me.

"I mean, could he be involved with the lab, somehow?" she went on.

"I doubt it. I think he's too young to be a lab technician, don't you?"

We fell quiet while we both thought.

"So what are you going to do?" Izzy asked eventually.

"I don't know."

"You want to tell Nancy? I mean, he probably *is* the intruder she was worried about."

"Yeah. He probably is," I agreed. "But I don't want to tell her. Not yet." I wasn't sure why. It was probably either the fact that we'd have to explain our unauthorized stakeout or not wanting to turn Max in before I knew exactly what he was up to — or perhaps a combination of the two. There was something stopping me; that was all I knew. "I've got an idea, though."

"Spill," Izzy said.

"How about I just find out from him?"

"From Max? What, like, ask him?"

I laughed. "Er, no. I can't see him happily sitting down and opening up about breaking into a strange lab in the middle of the night to some girl he's barely spoken to, can you?"

"What, then?"

"I follow him home after school. See what I can find out. If he really is the culprit, what does he want the crystals for? What's he doing with them?"

Izzy's eyes crinkled at the corners as she understood what I was saying. "And he won't even know you're there . . ."

"Because I'll be invisible!"

"Brilliant plan!"

And, yeah, OK, it *was* perhaps a brilliant plan. It felt bonkers and possibly risky, too, though. He wasn't exactly the kind of boy you wanted to annoy.

But it was the best option. I didn't want to tell Nancy about him until I knew what he was up to. She was expecting a full-on burglar, but Max was just a kid my own age. For whatever reason, I felt that I owed it to him to find out more before potentially landing him in a whole heap of trouble. I also wanted to figure out more about the way he'd looked at me. There'd been something in his eyes—as if we had something in common— and I needed to find out exactly what that was.

"All right, that's that, then," I said. "I'll follow him home today."

Chapter 14

I sat on the bus, five rows behind Max, and studied the back of his head. A messy, curly brown mop. It didn't really give much away. I looked out the window instead.

Just before the fourth stop, Max rang the bell and stood up. I followed him off the bus and walked along the streets behind him, keeping a respectful distance.

I felt like someone in a spy movie, trailing their mark without being spotted. Although, to be fair, it was a lot easier for me to do the not-being-spotted thing, given that I kept myself invisible for the entire time.

There was a slightly tricky moment when we got to his house. Max let himself in the front door so quickly I didn't have time to follow him inside.

I stood outside in the yard for a few minutes, staring at the closed door and wondering what to do. Then I had a stroke of luck. The door opened again. Max was in the doorway, rattling a box of cat food. "Spider!" he called.

Spider? Who calls their cat *Spider*?

Luckily, I was quicker off the mark than the cat. I saw it leap down from a tree in the front yard and head for the door. I squeezed through just before the cat did and slipped into the hallway seconds before Max pulled the door closed. I was in.

Now what?

I followed Max into the kitchen and watched as he put some food down for the cat. My head was full of questions. Where had he put the crystals? What was he going to do with them? How would I get out of here without being noticed, if I needed to?

And then something broke into my thoughts.

Max. Speaking. To me.

"I can hear you, you know," he said.

I looked around. There was no one else in the room. He *had* to be talking to me. But how could he hear me? I hadn't made a sound.

"Not out loud," he said. "Your thoughts. I can hear what you're thinking."

He could hear what I was *thinking*?

"Uh-huh. Every word. The closer you come, the more I hear."

I took a step back. And tried to stop thinking.

"Now I can hear you trying not to think," Max said. "And I know you're invisible, too, so you might as well uninvisiblize yourself and let's talk about this face-to-face."

Uninvisiblize?

"Yeah, I know it's not a real word. But, you know. Come on. Show yourself. I've told you I can read minds. You can turn invisible. So we're even."

Max was looking around the room as he talked, probably trying to figure out exactly where I was. I weighed my options. I could stand here and try not to think anything until he wondered if he'd imagined it and gave up—which didn't feel too likely. I could make a run for it—which didn't feel particularly clever since I'd come here to see what he was up to.

Or I could do what he said.

I focused on the empty part of my mind, filled it with thoughts and turned myself visible.

"You!" Max exclaimed, with what sounded like a mixture of disgust and annoyance.

"Oh, I'm so sorry I'm not someone more exciting," I said, folding my arms and doing my best to sneer at him. "You're not exactly my first choice to get caught up in a freaky situation with, either."

Max's mouth did something strange then. Well, it wouldn't be strange on most people, but it was strange on him. Mainly because I'd never seen him do it before.

He smiled.

At least, I think that's what it was. One side of his mouth didn't move; the other half twisted upward in a crooked tilt. "Fair enough, kiddo," he said. "You got me there."

Kiddo? Who was he calling *kiddo*? He was in the same year as me!

"Sorry," Max said. "It's just that you are small."

And he really was going to have to stop reading my mind.

"Sorry—again!" he said. "Look. Let's start over."

"OK."

"I've seen you around. What's your name anyway?"

I nodded. "Jessica Jenkins," I told him.

"Well, hi, Jessica Jenkins." He reached out a hand. "I'm Max," he said. "Max Malone."

I finally unfolded my arms and held my hand out to give his an awkward shake. "Hi, Max," I said. Something was whirring in my head, though. His name—where had I heard it before?

And then I remembered. Nancy! She'd said that the doctor she'd been working with was named Dr. Malone. Was it a coincidence?

"Malone," I repeated.

"You know my dad?" Max asked, reading my mind again.

"Do you have to do that?"

"Do what?"

"Hear my thoughts. Can't you stop?"

Max frowned. "Sorry. Believe me, it's worse for me than it is for you. Sometimes it's fun to read people's minds, but you don't always get to hear the most pleasant thoughts about yourself."

In his case, I could easily imagine that would be true.

"Thanks!"

Whoops. He'd done it again. I really was going to have to try to stop thinking so much. "I don't actually *know* your dad," I said, changing the subject. "But is he a doctor?"

Max pulled at his school tie to loosen it. "Yup," he said. "Dr. James Malone."

So I was right. Max was the doctor's son. And he had a superpower, like me. What did this all mean? How did he get it? Did the doctor know? Had he *given* Max the serum?

Max reached into a cupboard and pulled out a couple of glasses and some juice. "Want a drink?" he asked, clearly deciding to ignore the questions he'd probably overheard me thinking.

"Yeah, thanks."

He poured the drinks, and I followed him to the kitchen table.

Max took a long, noisy slurp of his juice. Then he wiped his arm across his mouth and looked at me. "OK," he said. "How about we start talking? You tell me your story; I'll tell you mine."

"OK. You first."

"Fair enough," he said. And I couldn't help a tiny dart of nerves shoot through me as he added, "If you're ready to hear about a whole lot of weird, I'll tell you everything I know."

"First and foremost, I'm not a thief," Max began.

"I never said you were."

"You were there the other night, though, weren't you? In the lab."

I hesitated for a moment.

Max nodded. "Thought so. I didn't notice anything until I was leaving."

"Till I was near enough for you to hear my thoughts," I mused.

"Yeah, probably. So if you were there, you'd have seen me looking at the crystals and stuff."

You were doing a lot more than looking at them, buddy, I thought.

"OK, not just looking at them," Max added, and I kicked myself and tried to remember to stop thinking.

"So if you weren't stealing them, what *were* you doing?" I asked.

Max shook his head. "To be honest, I dunno. Checking them out. Trying to figure out what's going on with me." He pointed at his head. "With this stuff."

"Yeah, I know what you mean."

"It only started a few weeks ago. Dad had been really busy." Max made a kind of sarcastic grunt. "Well, Dad's *always* busy. He's never been much of a hands-on kind of parent. I've always been clear about his priorities."

"Which are?"

Max ticked them off on his fingers. "Patients, hospital, more patients, more hospital, and then, maybe, somewhere down the line, me."

Despite myself, I felt a twinge of sympathy for him.

"Oh, don't start that!" Max snapped.

"Start what?"

"Feeling sorry for me. Woe is me and all that. Look, don't get me wrong. He's a great dad. He's always done his best, I know that. It's just— well, he's a doctor. It's like his calling, you know?"

"All right, I get it. No sympathy. Go on."

"OK. So, a couple of months ago, he started being gone even more. It was the anniversary of . . . well, it was kind of . . ." His voice trailed off. His cheekbones had flushed a tiny bit. Then he shook himself and carried on impatiently. "Anyway, something changed. Dad was still just as busy— in fact, more so—but his mood was different. He was kind of—I dunno—I want to say happier, but that's not quite right. He's never exactly happy. But he seemed to have more purpose, like something was driving him, exciting him in a way I couldn't remember having seen before."

"And this all started a couple of months ago?"

I asked. In other words, around the same time the doctor had approached Nancy and suggested they get back to work on the research.

"Yup."

"Did he say anything to you about it? Did you talk about it?"

Max laughed. It didn't feel like a real laugh. It was more of a sarcastic one, if you can laugh sarcastically. And maybe a little sad, too. "Dad actually communicate with me about something that mattered?" he said. "No, we didn't talk about it. We don't."

"You don't what?"

"Talk. That's just how it is. It's not a problem."

"So, what happened next?"

"I had to get in touch with him about a permission slip for a soccer tournament a couple of weeks ago. I assumed he was at work, so I called him at the hospital. I spoke to his secretary but he wasn't there. He wasn't at home, either. In fact, that was when I found out that he hadn't done a double shift for weeks. It shouldn't have bothered me. It was just another thing that I didn't have a clue about."

"But it *did* bother you."

"Yeah, it bugged the heck out of me."

"And I'm guessing you didn't think of the obvious solution?"

"Huh?"

"The one that would have involved the two of you having a conversation?"

"Ha, ha," Max said sarcastically. "No, I didn't do that. The more I thought about it, the more I found myself getting annoyed, and the more I wanted to know what he was up to."

I suddenly realized Max hadn't mentioned his mom yet, and I wondered if he meant he suspected his dad was having an affair or something.

"So, one day, I skipped school and followed him," Max went on in a rush, interrupting my thoughts. "I felt like I was in some kind of cheap spy thriller, hiding behind bushes and lampposts and dashing behind parked cars, wearing a pair of sunglasses to disguise myself from my own dad."

Yup, been there, done that.

"And he ended up at the lab."

"Had you been there before?" I asked.

"Nope. As far as I knew, he'd packed up his research years ago. But it turned out I was wrong. Seemed he was there every chance he got."

"And obviously you couldn't ask him why, due to the not-wanting-to-have-a-conversation thing."

Max frowned. "I took the only realistic option I had."

"You waited till he was at the hospital, then went over to the lab to find out for yourself exactly what was going on."

Max sat back and stared at me, as though he'd just noticed me for the first time.

"What?" My ears felt hot under his gaze.

"Not bad, kiddo," he said.

If he called me that again, I'd . . .

"Sorry, sorry!" He held up his hands in defense. "You're just smaller than me, that's all," he said. "And younger."

"How do you know?"

"I'm the oldest in the grade," he said. "I'll be fourteen at the beginning of September."

Which was when it hit me. Max's birthday wasn't the same as mine. He wasn't one of the two other babies born on the same day as me. We'd already established who they were. So *how* had he gotten this power?

I didn't want to disturb his flow. I needed to hear his story. "Carry on," I said.

"So, yeah, I wanted to go to the lab, but I couldn't go during the day. I'd already had two detentions that week. One more and there'd be a letter home, and under the circumstances, I didn't need that. So I set my alarm for ridiculous o'clock in the morning and sneaked out while Dad was asleep."

"And what happened when you got to the lab? How did you get in?"

"I'd spotted the keypad when I saw him there the first time and I'd planned ahead—made a list of all the significant numbers I could think of."

"And you got lucky."

Max looked at me, an unreadable expression on his face. It was like when a black cloud moves in front of the sun. Then it disappeared. "Yeah, something like that," he said. "I got into the lab, anyway."

I decided not to ask about the strange look. It didn't take the world's most intelligent person to realize that Max was not someone you discussed feelings with. "Then what?" I asked instead.

Max shrugged. "I wandered around, trying to figure out what was going on that had gotten my dad so excited. None of it made much sense to me. There were lots of sheets of paper with crazy formulas on them, crystals and jewelry all over the place, bottles and test tubes, machines that looked as if they'd come straight off the set of a sci-fi movie. But then something caught my eye."

"One of the crystals?"

"Yeah. Promise you won't tell?"

Could I promise that? Wasn't the whole point of this that I was finding out what was going on so I could tell Nancy?

"If it gets out, everyone'll think I'm a complete loon who needs to be locked up. Plus, my dad will kill me."

I knew how he felt. And even if he might not be the most pleasant person in the world, we were linked, and I felt a kind of loyalty to him already. "I promise," I said.

Max reached under his collar and pulled out something on a thin piece of black leather. A shiny, shimmering, silvery-black skull with a wide spooky smile, hollow holes for eyes, and two triangular slots for nostrils.

I leaned forward to examine it. "What on earth is that?"

"Well, it's called hematite, apparently. I've looked it up since. I didn't have a clue at the time, though. It was sitting in a pile of about fifty crystals—some on brooches and bracelets, others like little stones."

"Yeah, I've seen them."

"This little guy was sitting there, looking right up at me. Seemed to be smiling at me. I told myself Dad wouldn't miss one out of so many. Anyway, I planned to give it back at some point."

"So you stole it."

"So I *borrowed* it," Max said.

"And then what?"

"Then the mind-reading thing started happening. It was weird. At first it only happened when I was feeling tired. The first time was over breakfast. I was sitting there, half awake, eating my cereal. Dad was sitting across the table from me reading a medical journal, and then I heard it."

"What did you hear?"

"I heard my dad say, 'What a load of nonsense! I could have written this article ten times better.' Actually, he didn't say 'nonsense,' but you get the idea."

"I do."

"So I looked up from my cereal and asked him what he was talking about. He said he hadn't said anything. I said he had. He told me I was late for school and he was late for work. Then he folded up his paper and told me he was leaving in five minutes if I wanted a ride, and not to forget to brush my teeth."

"Gosh! I see what you mean about the level of conversation with your dad."

"I told you. Anyway, gradually, I realized that if my mind was kind of slow—you know, *empty*— the mind-reading thing would happen."

"And then you taught yourself how to deliberately empty a part of your mind but carry on as normal with the rest of it."

"I guess you've been there, huh?"

"Been there, got the T-shirt, the handbag, and the matching shoes and scarf," I said.

"Once I got my head around what was going on, and traced it back to the skull, I couldn't help wondering what the rest of it was about—what exactly my dad was up to in that lab."

"So you went back to the lab, 'borrowed' a few more crystals, and tried to put the rest of them to the test?"

"That's pretty much it, yeah."

"And I'm guessing what you found was that none of the other crystals had any effect on you?"

"You've tried it, too, huh?"

"Not exactly," I said carefully. I wasn't sure how much I wanted to tell him at this point, or if I should let him know about the experiments Nancy had shown us in the park. "What I do know is that it seems you only get one power—the one from the first crystal you use. After that, you can't swap or change it or add to it with another one."

"Yeah, that's the conclusion I'd come to as well. Hey, if I'd known that, I might have gone for one that gave me superhuman strength or something. Like I said, this mind-reading thing doesn't always tell you what you want to hear."

I was on the verge of thinking that he probably heard lots of people think unpleasant thoughts about him. But I stopped myself, for two reasons. For one thing, he'd know I'd thought it. And for another, sitting here talking with him like this, he didn't seem quite as bad as I'd thought. He was kind of OK, really.

Max gave me a scowl.

"You heard all that, didn't you?" I said as I realized it.

He nodded.

"Sorry."

Max shrugged. "It's OK. I'm used to it. So, anyway, that's my side of things. What's yours?"

I hesitated for a moment—and then I decided to tell him everything. What did I have to lose? Max was the only other person in the world like me—that I knew of. I had to trust him, and to be honest, it felt like a relief. I mean, I'd talked to Izzy about it all, and Nancy, and now we'd gotten Tom involved, and Heather, too. But at this point, Max was the only person who I *knew* had actually experienced having a superpower and would totally understand what I was going through.

He listened while I told him all about getting the necklace for my birthday and turning invisible in geography.

"That'll teach Cooper to be so boring!" he said with a laugh.

I told him about spying on his dad, and about meeting up with Nancy and seeing what the other crystals did.

"So that's how it works," he said when I told him about the bowl with the serum in it. "But why does it work on us? I've never drunk any of that stuff, as far as I know."

"I've no idea why it works on you," I said. I explained what Nancy had told me about getting the serum on me when I was a newborn. "Babies' cells are replaced much faster than adults' cells,"

I told Max. "Nancy thinks the serum must have affected me because of my cells multiplying so fast. But she says it stayed dormant in my body until now because apparently the brain has another growth spurt at our age, or something."

"That's good to know," Max said lightly. "Maybe mine'll develop enough that I'll stop failing chemistry one of these days."

I laughed. It felt nice. Nice to talk to Max and to share all this with someone who completely understood—which was probably why I decided to go a step further and tell him about the others.

"So there could be more of us out there," Max mused. "Any ideas who they might be?"

"Uh-huh," I said. "We think one is Tom."

"Tom? Tom who?"

"Tom Johnson. He's in my class. He's really—"

I didn't get any further as Max burst out laughing. "Little geeky math genius? *That* Tom? With a superpower? That's funny!"

My cheeks reddened as I felt a surge of loyalty toward Tom—and annoyance toward Max. Why did he have to be such an idiot at times?

Max stopped laughing. "You're right. I'm an idiot," he said. "Sorry. OK, who's the other?"

"Heather Berry."

Max tried to look uninterested but his eyebrows went up a little, as did the color in his cheeks. Typical. He probably had a crush on her, just like every other boy in our class.

Max glanced at me and folded his arms. "Anyway, moving on," he said quickly. "So you think they might have powers, too, but you don't know for sure?"

"Not yet. Izzy and I are hoping to meet them at lunchtime tomorrow. Hey, why don't you come, too?"

Max burst out laughing. "Yeah, right," he sneered.

"Oh. Sorry. Of course. You wouldn't be caught dead spending your lunch break in an art room with a bunch of losers when you could be out playing soccer with your friends."

Then he probably realized that Heather might be there as he unfolded his arms and shrugged. "I might show up," he said. "I'll see."

Which I took as an "OK, then," in Max-speak.

"Anyway," he went on, changing the subject. "It's even more of a mystery now. I wasn't born on the same day as you guys. As far as I know, I didn't get that serum stuff on me—unless my dad secretly gave me some and never told me about it! So why me?"

And I don't know if it was because we shared something completely crazy or because he was the kind of person I'd rather have as a friend than an enemy, or because I saw something in him that I guessed most people never got to see—a kind of vulnerability. Anyway, whatever it was, before I knew it, my mouth was doing that thing where it lets words come out without asking permission from my brain.

"I don't know," I said. "But from now on, we're in this together, and I'm going to help you find out."

Chapter 15

"Before we do anything else, we need a plan," I began. "And part one of the plan is that we need to take the crystals back to the lab."

"You're not turning me in!" Max said, shaking his head vigorously and folding his arms. "I'll deny everything. You can't prove it. I'll say you're making it up. I don't want people to know about this. They'll just call me a freak. My life'll be over."

I held my hands up in self-defense. "Max. Chill. I won't say anything. Like I said, we're in this together. We've got to trust each other. OK?"

Max gave me a sulky nod. "OK. Whatever."

"But we do need to put the crystals back. That way, Nancy will stop getting suspicious, and no one needs to know about you. You still have them, don't you?"

Max nodded.

"Can I see them?"

He paused for a moment, then got up from the table. "Hang on. I'll go get them."

A couple of minutes later, he was back with a small bag that he emptied onto the table. A rainbow of colors sparkled and winked as the sunlight hit them from the kitchen window.

I counted nine crystals. Three that looked like shiny pebbles, two that were like jagged pieces of rock—one bright red, the other deep green—two rings, a bracelet, and a pendant on a gold chain.

"I was never planning to keep them," Max said.

"I didn't say you were."

Then I remembered the other thing I'd seen. The bottle that he'd had in his pocket. "Is there anything else?" I asked.

Max looked as if he were about to deny it. Then he frowned. "You saw me, didn't you?" With a sigh, he reached into his pocket and pulled out the tiny bottle. He put it on the table with the crystals. "That's it," he said. "That's everything."

I picked up the bottle. "What *is* this?" I asked.

"I really don't know, but do you want to know something weird?"

"I'm *living* in the world of weird, so, yeah, hit me."

Max picked up the bottle. "OK, so I'd found this at the lab and it intrigued me. The other day, I was sitting at the table here, looking at it, and I opened it up and sniffed it to see what it smelled like. Just as I did that, Spider jumped onto my lap and bumped into the bottle."

"Your cat? Did it spill?"

"Yeah, about half of it went on the table."

"So what happened?"

"Before I even realized what was going on, Spider licked it up. Lapped it all up."

"Yikes."

Max frowned. "Yeah, that's what I thought. Or words to that effect, anyway."

"So then what happened?"

"Nothing at first. I watched him like a hawk. I was worried out of my mind in case anything bad happened to him. But he was fine. I didn't see any change—not till the next day, anyway."

"What happened the next day?"

"Spider was in a fight with another cat. I heard screeching and yowling and went to the back door to see what was going on. He ran in, fur sticking out like he'd been electrocuted, tail upright and as thick as a tree trunk. It took me a while to calm him down. He's only two and can be a bit of a bully, but he can be a real baby at times, too. Eventually he calmed down and I checked him over. He had a scratch on his paw, and it was bleeding all over the place."

"Poor thing."

"Yeah. Anyway, I took him into the kitchen to look for something to stop the bleeding. I grabbed a wad of paper towels, and I was going to wrap it around his paw." Max hesitated.

"So did it work?" I asked. "Did you manage to stop it?"

"That's just it. It wasn't bleeding anymore."

"Oh! Well, that's good, isn't it?"

"Mmm, I guess."

"You don't sound convinced."

Max leaned in and lowered his voice. "The cut, right? It was big and pumping out blood like a tap. But when I went to wrap it in the paper towels, it was gone. Disappeared, like it had never been there. And I mean *at all*. There was no cut and no sign that there had ever been one. The only way I knew I hadn't imagined the whole thing was that there were still spots of blood on the floor from where Spider had run into the house."

I tried to think. "Are you saying you think the serum had something to do with this?"

"That's exactly what I'm saying. See, I've been thinking about it, a lot," Max went on. "And I think I've got it figured out."

"Go on."

"OK, so the second time I went to the lab, I saw some sheets with names of crystals and notes on them. Most of them were full of question marks in the 'properties' column. But then I had a thought. I looked for a sheet that had any information on rubies."

"Why rubies?"

Max pointed at the cat. "Spider's got this ridiculously bling collar. He used to belong to my grandmother, who was a bit eccentric, extremely rich, and loved cats, especially Spider. The collar has an actual ruby on it. Just a tiny one, but it's real."

"So you thought that the ruby on the collar could have interacted with the serum?"

"Exactly."

"And? Did you find anything about rubies at the lab?"

"Yup."

"What did it say?"

Max looked me straight in the eye. "Heals wounds."

I stared at him as the breath whistled out of me. "Wow!" I said quietly. "I mean, a cat . . ."

"I know. Hard to get your head around, isn't it?" Max said. "Thing is, Spider gets into scrapes with the cats in this neighborhood fairly often. He comes home with scratches and bites on him at least once or twice a month, and the first time any of them have ever healed this quickly was the day after he'd drunk the serum. It *has* to have something to do with it."

My head was spinning. I barely knew what to think. "Max. Please, come tomorrow at lunchtime. If Tom and Heather are like us, that's two more people to help us figure all of this out. And even if they don't come, Izzy will be there, and she always comes up with good suggestions."

Max nodded. "OK," he agreed. Then he gestured at the crystals. "What about these?"

"We'll take them back together, OK? How about tomorrow night? Mom and Dad both go out on Wednesday evenings. I'll tell my neighbor I have to go out for a bit. She won't mind."

Max stifled a laugh. "You'll tell your *neighbor*?

I made a face. "I know. She checks in on me when my parents are out. Anyway, all she ever does is watch TV. She'll hardly notice I'm gone. So we take the crystals back tomorrow night, yes?"

Max clutched the cord on his neck. "I'm not parting with this one," he said. "Not now."

"I'm sure they won't notice if just one of the crystals is still missing," I said, compromising. "But we take all the others back. Maybe put them somewhere different—scatter them on the floor or something—so Nancy will just think they dropped them and didn't notice. They probably won't worry about yours too much as long as they've got all the others."

Max scowled. "Really? You think that'll work?"

"Have you got a better idea?"

Max shook his head. "OK." Then he smiled at me. "Thanks," he said.

I couldn't help thinking he wasn't too awful-looking when he smiled.

"Sometimes it's fun reading people's minds," he added shyly, and I felt my cheeks heat up.

We headed for the hallway. "What's your cell phone number?" Max asked. He got his phone out and punched my number in as I gave it to him, putting in my name as "J." I guess he

180

didn't want his tough-guy friends to tease him about being friends with a girl.

"I'll text you if I can't make it to lunch tomorrow, but I will try," Max promised.

"OK," I said. As I turned toward the door, I noticed a photo on the mantelpiece of a woman with a baby. "Is that your mom?"

Max looked at his feet. "Yeah," he mumbled.

"Aww, cute," I said, smiling. "Don't tell me that's you! I can't believe you were ever a sweet little chubby-cheeked baby!"

Max didn't reply. When he looked up, his face had clouded over. "I'll see you tomorrow, OK?" he said.

"Oh, OK, right," I faltered.

I stepped outside and turned to say good-bye, but he'd already shut the door.

And just when I'd been on the verge of thinking that Max Malone wasn't too bad after all.

I scarfed my snack as quickly as I could and went up to my room to call Izzy. She listened in silence to the whole story.

"That is totally awesome!" she said when I'd finished.

"Which part? The mind-reading boy, the self-healing cat, or the fact that Max Malone had a conversation with another human being that involved actual sentences and not just grunts?"

"All of it! This just gets better and better. And guess what! I finally pinned Tom down and made him talk to me. He says he'll come tomorrow at lunchtime."

"Great! How's he doing? Is he feeling any better about it all?"

"He's getting there. He said he's decided to treat it like an algebraic equation."

"How on earth does that work?" I asked.

"Well, he said that in algebra, you have to equalize two sides of an equation by matching up the quantities of the variables—or something."

"So he just has to establish how to match up potentially having a superpower with his fear of being even more different?" I mused.

"Exactly. Now that he's approaching it like a math problem, I think he'll be a hundred percent on board soon."

"That's a relief. I hated seeing him upset."

"Yeah, me too," Izzy agreed.

"Tomorrow at lunchtime, then," I said as my

stomach did a couple of cartwheels and a backward flip. One day from now, exactly how much
deeper into this crazy stuff were we all going to be?

On Wednesday at lunchtime, Izzy, Max, and I
sat in silence in the art room. Max said he was
there because he'd had nothing better to do. I
didn't really care what he said; I was just glad he'd
turned up.

I looked at my watch for the millionth time.
Twenty-five to one. Five minutes into lunch.

Max pushed back his chair and stood up.
"They're not coming, are they?" he said. "We're
wasting our time."

I opened my mouth to reply, but something
stopped me—a knock on the door, followed by a
face peeking around it. Heather!

"You came!" I burst out before I could check
myself and act cool.

She smiled shyly. "Can I come in?"

"Of course!" I shuffled up to make space beside
me and pulled another chair in.

I must have been right that Heather had already
discovered that she had a power of some kind—I

was sure of it now. Why else would she have agreed to spend time with someone she'd looked down her nose at for the last two years?

A moment later, there was another rap on the door. Tom stuck his head around and came in. "Sorry I'm late. I had to grab some lunch." He didn't meet anyone's eyes as he shut the door behind him and grabbed a chair. I guessed he was still feeling unsettled by it all. But he'd come, and that was what counted.

This was it, then. We were all here. It was time to get started.

While I was trying to figure out where to begin, Max got up and shoved a chair against the door handle. "So we don't get disturbed," he mumbled by way of explanation. Then he looked at me. As did the others.

I cleared my throat. "Um. OK, so thanks for coming," I said nervously. "Some of you might be wondering what this is about."

Tom looked down at his feet. Izzy smiled encouragingly. Heather's face didn't give anything away. Max tapped his fingers on his knee.

"OK, so, well, the thing is . . ." My voice trailed away. How on earth was I supposed to say all of this?

Max saved me. "Look, there's no point in beating around the bush," he said. And before I had time for one last change of mind about leaping into the unknown quite so spectacularly, he went on. "There's some weird stuff going on. It's top secret, and if you don't want to know about it or don't think it applies to you, then feel free to leave now."

No one moved.

"If you stay, you have to promise not to breathe a word outside this room," Izzy added. "Whatever is said from here on in is top secret. Agreed?"

"Agreed," Max and I said.

"Agreed," echoed Tom and Heather a little nervously.

"Good. All right." Izzy looked at me. "Back to you, then, Jess."

I paused while I tried to summon up the nerve. Then I decided we were halfway there already and so I might as well go ahead and jump off the cliff.

"OK, see, the thing is, we wanted to talk to you about some stuff," I began. "Weird stuff. Right now, it's only weird for me and Max—as far as we know." I paused for a moment and looked from Tom to Heather. "But we think that it might be weird for you, too. We think you're like us . . ."

185

Before I could say any more, Heather had gotten up from her chair.

"Wait! You're leaving?" I asked.

She shook her head. "I'm going to make this easier for you. There *is* something weird going on with me. I don't really know how to put it into words." She walked over to the corner of the room, turned back, and looked at us all. "So I'll show you instead."

She opened the door to a walk-in closet, full of paints, brushes, canvases, and crayons, went inside, and shut the door.

I looked around at the others. They were all staring at the closet door.

And then Heather came back into the room and the four of us gaped, openmouthed. See, there was one weird thing about the way she came back in.

She didn't open the door.

She walked through the wall.

Chapter 16

I stared at Heather. Then I stared at Max and Izzy. Then I allowed myself a glance at Tom, who seemed to have stopped looking awkward and nervous and instead was looking completely stunned. His mouth was so wide-open, I was concerned he might dislocate his jaw.

Max was the first to recover. I say "recover," but that might be an exaggeration.

"That—that . . . you . . ." was what he actually said.

Heather crossed the room and sat back down. She fiddled nervously with the edge of her sweater, then looked up at me. "You said something the other day that made me think you might be able to do this, too," she said. "Can you? Please tell me I'm not the only one. Tell me you've got some sort of explanation."

"You're *not* the only one," I said.

"Well, you're the only one who can do *that,*" Max put in. "That is a seriously awesome power!"

"So I *am* the only one?" Heather asked in a high-pitched voice.

I shot Max a look, then turned to Heather. "No. You're not." Then I took a huge breath and added, "We've asked you guys here because we think we all might have some kind of superpower."

"Well, not all of us," Max said, looking pointedly at Izzy.

Izzy blushed and looked down.

"OK, maybe not all of us," I agreed. "But Izzy is my best friend and she knows everything that's going on, and she's part of this, OK?"

Why was he being so difficult? As if this weren't hard enough already!

"I'm not being difficult," Max said, annoyingly reading my thoughts. "I'm just being honest."

"She never said you *were* being difficult," Heather told him, a confused frown scrunching up her forehead.

"No," Max said. "She didn't say it. She thought it."

"She *thought* it?" Heather laughed. "How on earth do you know what she . . . ?" Then she stopped. She looked from me to Max.

"Yeah," Max said. "I read her mind. That's what *I* do."

Heather mouthed the word "Wow!" although no sound actually came out.

She looked at me. "What can *you* do?"

"This," I said. Then I turned myself invisible. I watched Heather's face drain of color as I disappeared. I only stayed invisible for half a minute, then made myself visible again.

Tom broke the silence. "And you seriously believe that I could have one of these powers, too? I mean, as in actually for real?"

"Yeah, we do," I said.

Tom breathed out heavily through his nose, and nodded as if agreeing to a life-changing deal. Which, to be fair, wasn't too far from what he actually was doing. When he spoke again, he sounded like the main character in a film who was about to take the first steps on a new planet. Knowing Tom, he was probably imagining that *was* who he was.

"All right, let's do this," he said. "I want to find out."

"You're sure?" Izzy asked.

Tom nodded. "I haven't thought about anything else for the last two days. I need to know." He looked around at us and allowed himself a small smile. "And anyway, I don't need to worry about standing out. If I can really do something like you guys, then we'd be the same. I wouldn't be the odd one out at all. Come on, let's go for it. How do I do it?"

I smiled back at Tom, and, mainly to hide the fact that I suddenly had a lump in my throat, I started rummaging in my bag. I pulled out the cloth bag with the two crystals I'd bought at Tiger's Eye: the howlite and the turquoise. I opened it, picked up the crystals, and held them out for Tom to see.

"You need a crystal, like one of these." I pointed at Heather. "Heather's is . . . what was it again?"

Heather held out her hand to show us her ring. "Citrine."

I pulled my necklace from under my shirt. "Mine's rose quartz. Max's is hematite. Each one does something different."

Tom nodded seriously. "OK." He reached out an arm.

I stopped him. "Wait! Once you've used one and it works, that's the power you have. As far as we know, you can't swap it. That's it."

Tom tilted his head to the side and pulled at his thick curls. They bounced back up as he let go.

"No, that's not a moldy Life Saver," Max said. "It's a crystal."

"How did you know I was thinking . . . ?" Tom began. Then his eyes widened. "Oh, yeah. Jeez, that's pretty impressive."

"It's called howlite," I said.

Tom swallowed. "All right, then. I'll take it," he said.

"The howlite?"

"Uh-huh."

And before I could stop him, he'd taken the crystal out of my hand.

We all stared at him in silence.

"Tom, you shouldn't have done that," I said. "It could do *anything*. We haven't tested these. They could—"

"I'll be fine," Tom said. "Don't worry. There's something about this one. . . ." He turned the howlite over in his hands. "It feels kind of right for me, if that doesn't sound too stupid."

It didn't actually sound stupid at all. That was how I felt about my rose quartz. "Yeah, I know what you mean," I said.

"Me too," Heather agreed. Max gave a little nod as well.

Tom looked at the howlite in his palm. "OK, so that's all sorted out," he said. "Now what?"

Heather got up from her seat. "Wait a sec." She went over to the drawers by the window. She opened the top one, pulled out a ball of string and a pair of scissors, cut a length of the string, and brought it over to us.

She put her hand out for the crystal. Tom gave it to her and she threaded the string through the hole in the middle and handed it back to him. "Here," she said. "Put it on inside your shirt. Keep it next to your skin."

Tom took the string necklace from Heather, tied it around his neck, and tucked the crystal under his shirt. "Now what do I do?" he asked. "Nothing's happening."

"You have to relax," Izzy said. "Don't think about anything."

"Kind of empty your mind," I added.

"Empty my mind?"

"Yup," Max grunted. "Sounds crazy, doesn't it?"

Tom thought for a moment. "Not really," he said. "Some of the most important scientific breakthroughs in history have involved theories about emptiness. If quantum physicists can devote their lives to it, I'm sure I can spare a bit of my mind for it. I can try, at least."

We all waited in silence while Tom closed his eyes and tried to relax. Probably not easy with the four of us staring at him, watching for something to change.

Nothing happened.

Tom opened his eyes and frowned. "Hmm, OK, let me try that again," he said. He closed his eyes once more. This time, he took a couple of deep breaths and slowed his breathing down. We waited a full minute.

Still nothing.

"Maybe you're doing it wrong," Heather suggested carefully.

"It takes a while," I added. I hadn't really expected anything to happen right away. I mean, I'd had to practice for hours before I really got the hang of it. Mind you, this was Tom. He was the quickest person I knew at picking up a new skill.

Tom actually looked crestfallen. Maybe he'd been starting to like the idea of having a superpower after all. "Or maybe it's not going to work," he said. "Maybe the serum never got into my system. I should have known I wouldn't—"

"Do what you did at karate," Izzy interrupted.

Tom squinted at her.

"When you went to karate classes in elementary school, you said you had to do a kind of meditation thing before you began. Remember?"

"Oh, yeah. The teacher said I was the best in the class at it."

Izzy smiled. "Try that."

Tom closed his eyes. I watched him for thirty seconds. Then his eyes were open again—and he was beaming.

Why was he looking so pleased with himself when it hadn't worked—again? Maybe he was right after all. Maybe the serum *hadn't* ever gotten into his system.

"It's probably easier if you practice on your own," Heather suggested. "I could never have learned how to do it if I'd been trying in front of other people."

"And it'll take longer than half a minute," I added.

"I *gave* it longer than half a minute," Tom insisted. He was still grinning. "I gave it about two minutes. None of you moved. Wait. I know what I'll do. Are you ready?"

"Ready for what?" Heather asked.

"For . . . look, I'll show you." Tom turned to Max. "Max, what's on the table?"

"Er, nothing," Max said.

Had Tom lost it already? He couldn't see that the table was empty?

"OK. Now, observe." Tom closed his eyes and took in a slow, deep breath.

A moment later, his eyes were open. He *really* hadn't gotten the hang of this. I was about to say so when I looked at the table. It was full of stuff: books, paintbrushes, a vase of flowers, all our bags.

I pointed at the table. "What . . . ?" I said. "I mean, like, where . . . ?"

The others stared.

"How did you do that?" Izzy asked. "How did you get all those things on the table?"

Tom gave her a sly smile. "I can't be sure," he said. "But I think I stopped time."

❋

It felt like hours before we all stopped staring at Tom and found our voices.

"You . . ." Heather began.

"Stopped time. Yeah," Tom finished.

"But that's, I mean, that's . . . phew!" Max added helpfully.

"I spent all night practicing my power before I could do it that easily!" I protested.

Tom shrugged. "What can I say? I'm a quick learner." His smile was infectious. "You were right. I *am* like you guys! I have a superpower, too!"

The end-of-lunch bell stopped our celebrations. We had five minutes until afternoon classes began.

"When are we going to get together again?" Heather asked as we picked up our bags and quickly scarfed our lunches.

"Tomorrow at lunch?" I suggested. No one disagreed. "Great," I said, feeling a bubble of excitement at the thought of it. "See you all here again tomorrow, then."

"Looking forward to it," Heather said with another of those shy smiles.

"I can't *wait*!" Tom beamed as he pulled his bag onto his shoulder. He was himself again, only better. More confident. "I'm going to practice nonstop till then!"

Max laughed. "And, hey, see you this evening, Jess," he said, reminding me we still had to take the crystals back to the lab to keep Nancy from worrying about intruders. "Text me when you're on your way and I'll meet you on the bus."

"Will do."

As I headed into the afternoon's double history class, I couldn't help hoping that we weren't going to be learning anything too important. There wasn't the remotest chance of my concentrating on anything other than the crazy, the wild, the impossible, and the completely bizarre—aka my life.

Chapter 17

That evening, Max and I were crouched behind a hedge—the same one Izzy and I had crouched behind when we'd first spotted Max. It was beginning to feel like my special spot.

We'd spent the bus ride going over what had happened at lunchtime and planning what we were going to do now. We'd decided the best strategy was to put the crystals back in various random places where they could easily have been overlooked.

We'd been behind the hedge for ten minutes now, scoping out the street and waiting for the perfect moment—or, to be more precise, building up the nerve to break into Max's father's secret lab.

"There's no one around. The place is dead," Max said. "Plus, my knees are hurting. Come on. Time to go for it."

I had one more look down the street. Max was right. It was deserted.

"OK," I agreed. "You've got the crystals and the bottle with the serum?"

Max patted his pockets. "Yep."

"And you know the passcode?"

Max frowned. "I know it as well as I know myself," he said darkly.

"OK, good." I looked around one last time. "All right. Come on, let's go."

I stood up and was about to walk out from behind the hedge when Max grabbed me. "Wait!" he hissed. "Get back down!"

I instantly crouched back into position beside him. "What?" I hissed back. "What is it?"

"Look!" Max was pointing at someone. It was almost a repeat performance of the last time I'd been here, when Izzy and I had crouched down out of sight. Last time, it had been Max going into the lab. This time, I had absolutely no idea who it was.

From here, all I could see was a tall, slim man who seemed to be wearing a nice coat. He was definitely heading for the lab.

"Who's that?" I asked.

Max shrugged. "Can't really tell from here."

"Is it your dad?"

"No. He's too tall to be my dad."

I thought for a millisecond, then I knew what I had to do. "Max, I'm going in," I said.

"What do you mean, you're going in?"

I'd already closed my eyes. "Shh, I'm concentrating." A moment later, I'd turned invisible. "I'm going to follow him," I said. "See who he is and what he's up to."

"You can't! It's too dangerous."

I replied in a whisper. "He won't know I'm there," I said. "Just don't go anywhere, OK?"

"I won't," Max said.

"OK, give me the stuff."

Max took the bag with the crystals and the serum out of his pocket. He held his hand out, waving it around like someone feeling their way in the dark. I reached over and took the bag from him.

"OK, I'm off," I said. And before Max had a chance to talk me out of it, or I had a chance to freeze up with nerves, I was halfway down the road and heading toward the lab—and the stranger.

The first thing I deduced was that he clearly wasn't supposed to be there. He was fiddling with the keypad, trying different combinations. If he was part of the research work, surely he'd know the code. I studied his face as he entered numbers.

I didn't recognize him. His hair was short and neatly parted on one side. Even in the darkness, I could see that he had piercing blue eyes. So piercing, in fact, that when he looked around a couple of times and glanced in my direction, I felt positive he could see me. He couldn't, though. He wasn't acting like someone who knew they were being watched.

He was holding a notebook open at a page with various numbers on it. He tried a couple. Each time, the keypad made a buzzing noise and the door didn't open.

The man didn't seem to be getting ruffled at all. "You knew it wasn't that one," he mumbled. "Come on. You know the one to try."

He ran his finger down the page in his book. "This one," he said as he came to a number at the bottom of the page.

I watched him press the numbers: 0 . . . 6 . . . 2 . . . 6 . . .

The keypad beeped and the door clicked open. He'd done it. He'd broken in.

I put a finger in my mouth and bit on it to stop myself from gasping or making any other kind of noise that would have alerted him to my presence. Instead, I watched him calmly enter the lab, and before he had a chance to close the door behind him, I followed him inside.

The man peered curiously around the lab in a way that told me he hadn't been in here before. He wandered around, reading papers, sniffing the contents of bottles, examining the machines on the desks. All the time he did this, he was scribbling things down in his notebook.

Somehow, through my panic, I reminded myself what I was here for. The crystals.

I took the bag out of my pocket. Each time the man's back was turned, or he was busy making notes, I sneaked crystals into various places. I placed a couple of them under a table that had some others on top of it. I pushed them right up against the table leg, where they could easily have been missed. I put a couple more under some paperwork piled high on a desk. Again, it would have been easy enough to have missed those.

I still had three crystals in my hand. I peered around the lab for another hiding place. Then I spotted a cardboard box, half open, on the floor under the far desk. Only problem was, the man was standing right next to it. I held my breath and waited for him to move. As soon as he'd crossed over to the other side of the lab, I crouched down, sneaked under the table, and dropped the remaining crystals into the box. They could easily have slipped off the table into that.

Now there was just the serum to return.

I was tiptoeing across the lab to the cupboard it had come from when the stranger suddenly stepped backward, right into my path. I jumped sideways, knocking a pile of papers off the desk as I did.

The man spun around. "Who's that?" he snapped. His voice sounded like a hiss.

I stayed as still as I had stood the time I'd been desperate to win freeze dance at Izzy's seventh birthday party. For good measure, I stopped breathing, too.

The man bent down to pick up the papers. "Concentrate, man," he said to himself. His voice was deep and menacing. "Make a mess and they'll know you were here."

Phew. He'd assumed he'd disturbed the papers himself. I managed to breathe out.

The man continued snooping around the lab. With every step he took, I was more and more convinced he was going to discover me. Plus, he was right in front of the cupboard I needed to get into. Any second now, he'd open it and see the vials that contained all the ready-made serum. No!

He was reaching up toward the cupboard and I was wondering how I could distract him without giving myself away when the sound of an old-fashioned telephone broke the silence.

The man patted his jacket pocket and pulled out a cell phone. "What?" he said, his voice low and deep and menacing. He paused for a moment, then spoke: "Yes, yes, of course I did. . . . No, not yet . . . I just need a bit more time."

I put my hands in my pockets to stop them from shaking. My fingers tightened around the bottle of serum. I had to put it back.

"Yes, I know that it's a lot of money, and, as I said, you will get it all back. With interest. I take my business dealings seriously, and I have never defaulted on a loan. . . ." There was another pause before he added, "I'm pursuing a new lead."

The man turned vaguely in my direction and smiled. It was a predator's grin. Then he nodded impatiently. "Believe me, you'll be more than satisfied. I'm going to invent the most incredible thing. . . . Let's just say I've got a winning formula."

At that point, he broke off to chortle at his own

joke. His laugh cut through me as if it were a steak knife and I was dinner. "Trust me," he continued. "Just give me more time, and I will make you almost as rich as I'm going to make myself."

Then, in a voice that was so slimy it was as if a snake were slithering out of his mouth with his words, he added, "Of course I'll test it rigorously. . . . On whom? I don't know—a bunch of kids who don't demand to read contracts or be paid. I'll find them from somewhere."

OK, that was it! I had to get out of here. My fingers loosened around the bottle in my pocket. I'd managed to put everything else back. It was only one little bottle. Surely no one would miss that. I couldn't risk staying here another minute.

Luckily, a few minutes later, the man walked close enough to the automatic door that it whooshed open. I took the opportunity and whizzed through. As it slid shut, I opened the front door as quietly as I could, edged outside, and softly closed it behind me.

And then I ran like the wind, back along the path, back to Max, back to safety.

It was only once I'd made myself visible again and we'd sneaked back down the road and into the relative security of the town center that I finally stopped shaking and allowed myself to ask the questions I was pretty sure we were both thinking.

Who *was* that man? What was he doing breaking into the lab? Did he know about the crystals and our superpowers? And, if so, what exactly was he planning to do with them—and with us?

Max's face was white as we sat on the bench at the bus stop. Anyone would have thought *he* was the one who'd nearly gotten caught breaking into a lab while invisible.

I told him everything I'd seen and overheard.

"He wants children to experiment on?" Max said numbly.

"Well, he didn't exactly use those words. But, yeah, that was the impression I got."

"Do you think he knows about us?"

I shook my head. "I don't think so. He was too vague about getting kids to help him. I think he'd have been more specific if he'd meant us."

Max sighed. "Well, that's something, I guess. But what *does* he know? What's he even doing here?"

"And, more important, who the heck is he?"

Max looked up, as if he'd only just remembered I was there. "You know, I—I think I might have an idea," he said.

"You know him?"

Max shook his head. "I don't know him. But . . ."

"But what?"

Max swallowed. "But I think I've seen him before."

"Who is he?"

"I'm not sure. He told me he was a friend of my dad's."

For a second, I let myself feel relieved. So he *wasn't* some weird psycho stranger after all. He was a friend of the doctor and probably had every right to let himself into the lab, even if he did do it in the middle of the night and sneaked around like a thief.

Like I said, I only felt relieved for a second. Because then Max added, "But I think he was lying."

"Tell me everything," I said.

"It was the first time I went to the lab," Max began. "I'd just left and was walking down the road when I saw him. He seemed to come out of nowhere, and it made me jump."

"Go on."

"He came over to me and apologized for startling me. I wanted to get away, but he drew me into conversation. I felt a bit awkward, 'cause I wasn't sure if he'd seen me come out of the lab and if he knew I wasn't supposed to be there. I kept talking to him just to make sure I didn't come across as suspicious. We walked along the road together. He was really friendly. Said he'd known my dad years ago and was hoping to get back in touch."

"That all sounds innocent enough."

"Yeah, that's what I thought, too. He didn't want me to mention anything to Dad, because he was going to surprise him. They were old friends and went back a long way, he said." Max's voice trailed off and he looked down at his feet.

"What is it?" I asked. "Did he say anything else?"

Max nodded. "He said he knew my mom. It was the only part of the conversation that seemed a bit strange."

"Strange how?"

"He was talking about a time before I was born, maybe kind of overdoing it with how well he'd known my parents and how friendly they'd been. He told me how he'd been to a surprise birthday party for my mom once. Then he broke off and

208

suddenly exclaimed, 'Of course! That's it!' I asked him what he was talking about and he got flustered and said he'd just remembered he had to be somewhere."

"Couldn't you tell what he was thinking?" I asked. "Read his mind?"

Max shook his head. "I'd only just gotten the hematite. I hadn't worn it yet."

"So then what happened?"

"Nothing! He rushed off to his appointment, and I didn't really give him another thought until now." Max turned to look at me. His face had drained of color. "Jess, it was when he mentioned my mom's birthday that he suddenly got strange and then disappeared on me."

"Um. Yeah. And?"

"The combination on the keypad," Max said quietly.

"Zero-six-two-six?"

Max nodded. "It's a date. The twenty-sixth of June." He looked down at his feet and added in such a quiet voice I could barely hear him over the sound of the approaching bus. "Jess, I think it was talking to me that made him realize how he could break in! The twenty-sixth of June . . . it's my mom's birthday."

Chapter 18

The next morning, I was waiting for the bus and mulling over everything that had happened when a car startled me out of my thoughts. I looked up. Nancy. She pulled over and lowered her window.

"Jess, get in," she called, leaning over and waving me over. "I'll take you to school."

I looked over my shoulder, feeling like a spy in an action film. Then I realized two things. Thing one: Nancy was a close family friend, and there was nothing remotely suspicious or spy-like about her giving me a lift to school. Thing two: there were four other people at the bus stop, two of whom were talking about hairstyles so animatedly that there wasn't the slightest chance they would be aware of anything else going on around them, and the other two were totally engrossed in their phones.

So I got in the car.

"What's up?" I asked, concentrating very hard on making my voice sound casual and relaxed, neither of which I was feeling, as I pulled the door closed and fastened my seat belt. My brain was working overtime, trying to figure out how she'd found out about Max, if she knew we'd been to the lab last night, and exactly how much trouble we were in as a result. Turned out I didn't need to worry.

Nancy pulled out onto the road and glanced at me. "I wanted to tell you," she said brightly. "I went to the lab first thing this morning."

First thing? I checked the clock on her dashboard: quarter past eight. Surely *this* was first thing.

"I'm an early riser," Nancy said, noticing my look of confusion. "That's what happens when you do too many night shifts. Anyway, I couldn't sleep; I was worrying so much about the lab. So I decided to go down there and have a really good look around, and guess what!"

"What?" I asked, trying to inject the perfect

I-have-no-idea-what-you're-going-to-tell-me-because-obviously-I-was-nowhere-near-the-lab-last-night tone into my voice.

"It's all there!"

"The crystals?"

"Yes! Well, actually, I haven't found them *all* yet. There are one or two still unaccounted for—but I looked everywhere and found most of them. James must have knocked them off the table or covered them with his notes without realizing. But the great thing is, it was just an oversight. No one's been breaking in." She smiled broadly. "Isn't that great?"

"Yay! That's awesome," I forced out of my mouth with as much surprise as I could muster. We'd done it! We'd gotten away with it. Max wouldn't get into trouble. I was surprised at how glad I felt for him.

"I've also changed the keycode, just to be on the safe side. I should have done that earlier, but I didn't want to do anything to unsettle James while I was unsure," she went on as she drove. "Now that I know no one's coming in, I feel happy to tell him it's just a routine thing to keep on top of security. Anyway, we're safe. I'm so relieved!"

"That's wonderful news," I said. And it was,

actually. We weren't in any trouble—which meant I was almost as happy and relieved as Nancy.

"I don't know what we would have done if the project had come under threat now," Nancy went on. "I dread to think what would have happened if all of this had gotten into the wrong hands. Can you imagine?"

Er . . . yes, actually. I'd done little *but* imagine what could happen. I'd practically felt the bars of the experimental cage that I was trapped in while scientists prodded and poked me. I'd seen the newspaper front pages with "Jessica Jenkins—Freak of the Century!" splashed across them. I'd imagined that horrible creepy man from the lab giving horrible creepy orders about what to do with us.

"The tiger's eye, for example," Nancy continued. "Imagine if some really bad people got hold of an innocent-looking crystal that could become a bomb!" Nancy shivered. "It's unthinkable." She turned to smile at me. "But, thankfully, we don't *have* to think about it. No one's breaking into the lab. We're safe."

"Yay," I said weakly. Part of me really, really wanted to tell her about the man. I knew I probably should. But I'd promised Max I wouldn't betray him, and how could I tell Nancy about the man without giving Max away? My greater loyalty was to him right now. I couldn't break my promise. Not yet.

"This is the first time James has been happy for years," Nancy said, making me even more determined not to tell her. "It's as if he has something to live for again. I couldn't bear the thought of him going back to the state he had been in for so long."

"What made him so unhappy?" I asked.

Nancy checked her mirror and changed lanes. "It's a long story," she said.

It wasn't even 8:20 yet. I didn't have to be at school till quarter to nine. "I've got time."

Nancy stopped at a traffic light and then turned to me. "It started with his wife."

His wife. Max's mom. "What about her?" I asked.

"Rachel had a rare genetic disease. She'd lived with it for years, but it had begun to spread through her body at an alarming rate. The awful thing was that she was pregnant when this happened, so the doctors didn't want to use aggressive treatment to fight the disease."

Pregnant . . . with Max?

"The doctors pretty much gave up on fighting her illness," Nancy went on. "All except for

James. We'd gotten to a really important stage with our research, and he was positive he could use it to help her."

"So he tried the serum on his wife?"

Nancy nodded. The light turned green, and she set off again. "Not that it did anything. But she held on. Managed to carry her baby to full term. A beautiful little boy."

I stifled any response. I wondered if Nancy had met Max lately, and whether she'd still describe him as a beautiful boy.

"I think it was little Max who kept her going. But just before his first birthday, she started to go rapidly downhill. James had been working around the clock on the serum. We'd added a few ingredients and changed the percentages a bit. We really thought we were onto something."

Nancy took a left and turned onto the long road that runs parallel to the river all the way up to school. "Rachel was starting to slip away," she carried on. "Her doctors said it would only be a matter of weeks. James was desperate. He never slept—just spent all day by her side and all night doubling his efforts on the serum. It was a powerful medicine, and we decided, together, that we would try this latest version of it on Rachel."

"Did the hospital know that he tried the serum on his wife?"

"Good grief, no. He'd have lost his license on the spot."

"But he still did it."

"He would have done *anything* for her. Anything to make her better. I was there, and I can still picture the scene as if it were yesterday. The way James sat with her and held her as she sipped it . . ."

"And what happened?"

"Not a thing. In fact, that night she went downhill even more quickly. It was their wedding anniversary the next day. James had bought her a stunning necklace. She was so thin that she hadn't been wearing her jewelry for months. Nothing fit anymore. James wanted her to feel beautiful again."

I felt a twitch of something itchy running along my skin, making the hairs on my arms prickle. "What kind of necklace was it?" I asked.

"A beautiful pendant—a multicolored stone. Stunning. It was a black opal."

My brain was whirring even faster now. The serum. A brand-new pendant with a precious stone in it . . .

"Rachel put the pendant on—and something incredible happened. She sat up in bed for the first time in months. She talked lucidly for the first time in weeks. She had a conversation with both of us. We laughed together. Then she started saying strange things."

"Like what?"

"She said she could hear the wind—which was impossible, as we were on a ward in the center of the hospital. Plus, there was barely a breeze that day, but Rachel was convinced she could hear it."

Nancy glanced at me and continued. "And there was more. Rachel looked up at the ceiling and said how beautiful it was, how many different shades of white she could see in it. Stroked James's hand and told him she could feel the lines on his palm so strongly she half thought she might try reading his future from it. He said he could read his future himself, and that she was in it."

"That's so romantic," I said.

"Yeah."

We were approaching school. Still fifteen minutes early. Nancy signaled and pulled over down the road from the school gates. Then she cleared her throat. "Rachel died that night."

I felt hot tears behind my eyes. "I'm sorry,"

I said. I wasn't just sorry for Nancy. I was sorry for Max. It all made sense now. His tough-guy image — and the fact that it wasn't really convincing. I winced as I remembered my comment about the photo in the hall at his house. No wonder he'd been irritated with me after that.

"Is that why you said the serum might be dangerous for adults to drink?" I asked.

"Yes. We didn't know it at the time, but we deduced later that if your brain is no longer in the developmental stage, taking the serum can speed up the multiplication of cells, which is highly dangerous."

"And you think that's what happened to Max's mom?"

Nancy nodded. "James gave up on almost everything after Rachel died. His whole world caved in. He threw away every drop of the serum that he could find. All of it gone, apart from twenty bottles or so that I'd kept at home. James tore up and burned all the notes on the serum," Nancy continued. "Deleted all the computer files. Threw away everything he could find that reminded him of it."

"Why?"

"He couldn't forgive himself for what had

happened; he blamed himself for Rachel's death — for getting it so wrong. And then, once he'd gotten rid of everything to do with the old serum, he started again from scratch."

"Huh? He went back to his research?"

"James didn't want Rachel's death to be in vain. Trying to find a cure for the illness she'd had was the only thing that gave his life any meaning."

"What about his son?" I prompted.

"Yes, of course, poor Max. James loved him, but he wasn't the best father in those days."

Or *any* days, judging by some of the things Max had said.

"He invested all his time in his research. He felt that if he could somehow make a breakthrough, perhaps Rachel's death would have some meaning. Then one day he made the mistake of saying too much to the wrong person." Nancy twiddled with her hair. "Remember I told you we were government-funded?"

"Uh-huh."

"Well, James and I had become friendly with the man from the department who'd granted the funding — Oscar Finch. James and Oscar would go out drinking together — too much drinking, if you ask me, but at least it gave James someone to talk to. A friend whom he could confide in and trust. At least, that was what we thought at the time."

"OK."

"One night, after downing half a bottle of whiskey, James told Oscar what he'd done with the original serum, how he'd given it to Rachel. And he told Oscar what had happened."

"Yikes. Did he lose his job?"

"Far from it! James got a message from Oscar the next morning asking him to come and see him. After the conversation they'd had the night before, James was convinced he was about to get sacked, but Oscar had different ideas. He believed we were on the verge of a modern miracle."

"Really? But that's good, isn't it? So he was happy for you to carry on with the research?"

"Not exactly carry on with it. He wanted us to go back to the *original* research. He wanted us to re-create the serum James had given his wife. Not just that, but he wanted us both to leave our jobs, take the whole thing out of the public sector, and run it with him as a private scheme."

"I don't understand. What does that mean?"

"It means that the research would no longer have been about medical advances. It wouldn't have been about trying to find ways to cure the very sick and heal the unhealable. Instead, it would have become about developing a magic trick on a scale the world had never seen before—and selling it to the highest bidder. All Oscar saw was a magic potion that somehow enhanced people's senses and gave them capabilities beyond anything anyone had ever heard of."

"I see."

"A medicine that could make you hear things happening a mile away, see things previously invisible to the human eye? Well, Oscar's eyes just saw dollar signs—and lots of them," Nancy went on angrily. "His idea was that we could develop it into the perfect weapon to sell to the world's armies, the perfect spying tools to sell to intelligence agencies across the globe, the perfect product to make aging people feel younger. Basically, the perfect anything that would make him rich." She paused for a second to take a breath. "Oscar didn't care about medicine, about people's well-being. All he cared about was getting rich and becoming powerful—no matter what it took or who it hurt."

"I'm guessing Dr. Malone said no?"

"Darn right he said no! His medical research had *never* been about money or glory. Those things meant nothing to him, and they meant even less after he lost Rachel."

"And how did that go down?"

Nancy laughed sadly. "They had a massive argument. James finally got it through to Oscar that he would *never* use his research to pursue gimmicks, egos, and money. Surprise, surprise—within a week our funding was cut and James was ordered to submit his final report and ditch the project. He had to sign a contract agreeing that he'd never go back to it."

"Jeez."

"Yeah. So that was that. To be honest, at that point, James had lost all his fight anyway, and the research had more or less stalled. So we packed up our stuff and went back to our day jobs. James worked every shift he could to make sure he kept the house and gave Max everything he needed. Max was all that mattered to him."

I thought about the way Max had described his dad's double shifts. As if the *hospital* were what mattered to him. Turned out he couldn't have been more wrong.

"And what happened to Oscar Finch?"

"I've no idea. He probably found some other sucker to make him rich."

I thought for a moment. "So I'm guessing this guy is the one you meant by 'the wrong hands,' then?"

Nancy turned to me. "He's a dangerous man, Jess. You don't know how relieved I was to find the crystals this morning. If Oscar found out about any of our latest research . . ."

She didn't need to finish her sentence. I'd probably already pictured all the worst things she could imagine. Not only the tabloid headlines and the experimenting cage; now I also had a picture of me being sold off to the highest bidder and used by terrorists in some kind of superpowered war.

Nancy glanced at me. "Hey, there's no need to look so scared," she said. "We haven't seen Finch for years. He's completely out of the scene—and no one's been breaking into the lab." She reached out to pat my hand. "There's really nothing to worry about."

We'd been sitting down the road from the school gates for ten minutes. It was time to go. But I couldn't move. Something was bugging me, and I couldn't ignore it. I didn't want to ask, but I knew I had to . . .

"Nancy," I said nervously. "What did he look like?"

"Finch?"

"Uh-huh."

Nancy allowed herself a smile. "You know, I had quite a crush on him when we first met him. He was so handsome. Over six foot tall, immaculate sandy hair—always combed and parted to perfection—and the bluest eyes you've ever seen."

My gut did a backward somersault. "Blue eyes?" I asked, trying to keep my voice steady.

"Yes—so intense you felt he was seeing right into your soul when he looked at you."

"Mm-hmm," I murmured. I couldn't trust myself to say anything else. I swallowed hard. Eventually, I found my voice. "And how did he dress?" I asked.

"Oh, he was the sharpest person you've ever met. You could wear your best clothes and you'd still feel scruffy next to him. In fact, I don't think I ever saw him out of a shirt and tie. Nice dresser. Smooth talker. An evil, cold, and calculating person." Nancy stopped and looked at me. "Jess, are you OK? You've turned white."

"I—I just realized I'm late," I said. What else could I say? I couldn't tell her. I *couldn't*. She was so happy that everything was resolved at the lab. The doctor was happy, too. She'd already told me how good he was feeling now that he was working on his research again. I couldn't take it all away from them. And I couldn't betray Max. But what *could* I do?

All I knew was I had to get away. I needed to find Izzy and Max and tell them the news — that I was almost positive I now knew who we'd seen at the lab last night.

And that things were about as bad as they could possibly get.

Chapter 19

Except, as it happened, I was wrong about that. It turned out things could get much, much worse.

I started looking for Max as soon as I got through the school gates. We still had five minutes till the bell rang for homeroom, and I was sure he'd be in the athletic field next to the school yard, hanging out with his soccer friends near the goalposts.

But he wasn't with his soccer friends.

I searched for him when the bell rang and we formed lines for our classes. I was sure he must be at the back of his line.

But he wasn't in line.

I darted out of homeroom as soon as Ms. Forshaw finished taking attendance then I ran along the hall to his homeroom and peered through the window.

He wasn't in the classroom.

He wasn't anywhere. He wasn't at school.

I bumped into Izzy in the corridor outside Mr. Martins's classroom. We had English first thing. "Iz, Max isn't here," I breathed.

Izzy looked at me blankly. "So? He's probably just late. Or home sick."

I hadn't had time to fill her in on everything Nancy had told me, so she had no way of knowing why I needed to see him so urgently.

"Are you OK?" she asked.

"I'll tell you everything when we meet up at lunch, but I need to speak to Max as soon as I can," I said. "Can you tell Mr. Martins I'm going to be late? Think of a good excuse."

"Of course. I'll tell him you've got a bad headache and you've gone to see the school nurse."

"Perfect," I said, already turning away and getting my phone out. "I'll be there as soon as I've made contact with Max."

Except I didn't make contact with him. I phoned. No answer. I texted. No reply. Finally, I gave up and went to English, clutching my head to make my excuse seem authentic.

I faced the front and did my best to concentrate on the lesson. It wasn't easy. My mouth was saying things like, "Yes, Mr. Martins, it's a really good poem and I like the way the poet uses metaphors and similes," but my head was busy wondering what on earth had happened to Max and where all of this was going to lead.

At lunchtime, Izzy and I headed up to the art room to meet the others. I filled her in on everything as we walked. Maybe Max would already be there.

He wasn't.

"I'm really worried, Iz," I said as we entered the art room. The others weren't there yet. "I'm afraid there's something seriously wrong. I just don't think he would ignore all my calls and not turn up at school if everything was OK."

"I don't know. There's probably a logical explanation," Izzy said. "Let's not assume the worst yet."

Izzy had a point. A week ago, Max hadn't even known my name. Who was I to say that keeping an arrangement with us was going to be his number-one priority now? "You're right," I agreed. "I'm blowing things out of proportion. I'm sure there's nothing to worry about."

Which was the moment my phone pinged to say there was a message from Max.

And it turned out that we did have something to worry about, after all. In fact, we had quite a lot to worry about.

I clicked on Max's name to open the message. In big letters at the top of the screen were the words "Max has sent you a video using Hula! ☺." Beneath that was a square box with a big arrow on it and the message "Click HERE to see the video." Izzy shuffled closer so she could watch as I clicked on the arrow.

After a few moments, Max's face appeared on the screen. He was sitting on a chair in a room that looked like an office. I didn't recognize it. I hit PLAY.

Max stared woodenly at the camera. Then he turned to talk to someone offscreen. "Do you want me to start now?" he asked. There was a muffled reply. Max turned back to the camera.

"Hi, J," he said. That was the name he'd used for my contact on his phone. Did that mean the video was only being sent to me?

"J?" the off-camera voice questioned.

"Yeah, J. James. My dad. It's my nickname for him," Max replied, looking away from the camera.

Huh? So it *wasn't* aimed at me? It was meant for his dad—but why had *I* gotten it, then? And did he *really* use the same name for his dad that he used for me?

The voice mumbled something else.

"OK. Hi, Dad," Max began again. "So, I know you'll be surprised to get this message," he went on. "In fact, you'll probably be wondering if it's actually meant for you." As he said this, his eyes narrowed. He moved his hand around his neck—where his necklace usually was. But it wasn't there! Maybe he wanted whomever was watching to know he didn't have it? Then *was* the video meant for his dad, or was it secretly aimed at me?

"But it's definitely meant for you," he said, looking directly at the camera. "I'm your kiddo."

Kiddo! That's what he'd called *me*! The message *was* meant for me! But for some reason, he had to pretend he was sending it to his dad. I kept listening, and watching out for more clues.

"So, here's the thing. I've kind of been kidnapped."

Kidnapped?

"Don't say that!" the voice off camera said.

"OK, scratch that," Max went on. He stood up from his chair. "As you can see, I'm not being tied up or beaten or treated particularly badly. I've even been fed—quite well, actually. I have, however, been locked in a room and told that I can't leave until you do what is required." Again, Max looked so hard at the camera that I felt certain the message was aimed right at me. "So you must follow these instructions," he said firmly. "You understand that, don't you?"

Did I understand? I was fairly sure I did. He was probably supposed to have sent the video to his dad, but had somehow managed to send it to me instead. He didn't want his dad to know what was going on—either because he didn't want to worry him or because he didn't want to run the risk of his dad finding out about his superpower— which made total sense to me, either way. But he needed rescuing, and he was putting his trust in me. Well, I wouldn't let him down.

"Oh, and sorry if you've tried to get hold of me," he added. "I've only just been given my phone back to do this."

The camera seemed to shake, and Max's face went blurry. Then the other voice came again. "Let me talk to him," he said. Max moved out of the way and someone else appeared on the screen. Someone I'd already seen once in real life. The last person I ever wanted to see again.

Oscar Finch.

Finch sat on the chair, smoothed down his hair (which was already perfectly smooth), straightened his tie (which was already perfectly straight), and smiled a smarmy, creepy smile into the camera.

"Hello, James," he said, smooth as melted chocolate. "Long time no see. Sadly. Not my choosing. So, anyway, I thought it would be nice to get together again. How about we meet at your lab? You know, the one you opened secretly. The one where you're working on the research you refused to continue working on with me. The research that you were then banned from ever returning to. Remember?"

Finch's voice had grown tighter, angry. He cleared his throat, straightened his tie, and smiled at the camera again.

"Why don't we say six o'clock tonight? I'll see you at the lab. Max will be staying here, but don't worry, I won't hurt him. At least, not if you give me everything connected with your research." Finch leaned toward the camera. "I want it *all*," he said in a voice so full of menace and threat it sounded as if it had metal arrows pointing out of it.

My whole body shivered as he continued.

"Of course, it's completely up to you whether you choose to hand over your research or not, just as it's completely up to me how I decide to deal with your son. Personally, I've always enjoyed those films where people find themselves becoming extremely helpful as they watch their loved ones screaming in agony."

Finch sat back in his chair and grinned. It was the smile of a snake. "So, you better get yourself down to the lab tonight," he said in a voice as cool and casual as if he'd been inviting a good friend to come out to play golf. "It's been a while. It's time we talked."

With that, Finch got up out of his seat and walked toward the camera. The last thing I saw was his hand reaching out. Then there was a click and the screen went blank.

We stared at the dark screen. I didn't know what to think. I couldn't swallow. I couldn't speak. I could barely breathe.

Izzy turned to me. "Jess, this is bad," she said.

"It's *really* bad," I agreed.

"What are we going to do?"

"I have no idea."

"Call the police?"

I shook my head. "I don't think Max wants us to do that. If he'd wanted to go through official channels, he'd have sent the message to his dad like he was supposed to."

"You're right," Izzy agreed.

"I think he sent it to me because he wants us to rescue him."

"I think so, too."

"Only question is—how on earth are we supposed to do that?"

As if in reply, the art-room door suddenly burst open and Tom ran in. "Sorry I'm late," he said. "I just had to tell the Math Olympics team I'd join them later for the marathon practice session."

He grabbed a chair and sat down. His worried demeanor from earlier in the week was completely gone. The old Tom was back, thank goodness. We might be needing him.

The door opened again.

"Sorry!" Heather was breathless as she came in. "Had to go to see Ms. Green about Saturday's volleyball tournament. I got away as soon as I could."

Despite everything else that was going on, I had

a tiny moment of happiness that Heather had cut short talking about her precious volleyball to be with us. And that Tom had given up time at his favorite thing in the world.

"What have I missed?" Heather asked as she pulled up a chair and took out her sandwich.

Izzy and I looked at each other. How were we supposed to answer that?

Izzy grimaced. "Max has been kidnapped," she said.

"What?" Tom gasped. "Kidnapped? How? When? By whom?"

"It's probably just a prank," Heather said dismissively. "You know what he's like."

I thought through what I'd learned about Max in the last couple of days: how he'd lost his mom as a baby; how he'd never gotten enough attention from his dad, because the doctor had buried himself in his work to deal with his grief; how gentle Max had been with his cat. And finally I thought about the look on his face in the video — the look of a scared little boy.

"Max might not be the nicest person in the world, but he has his reasons," I said. "And it's not a prank." I got my phone out and clicked on the link again. "Watch." The others crowded around.

When the video ended, I filled them in on everything else. Last night's trip to the lab, what I now knew about Max—and about his kidnapper, Oscar Finch. "We've got to save Max," I finished.

Heather nodded. "Agreed. But how?"

"That's what we have to figure out," I said hopelessly.

Tom cleared his throat and leaned forward. "OK, let's look at the facts," he said. "Max has been kidnapped by a guy who used to work with his dad and who wants to experiment—possibly on children—so that he can make millions of dollars for himself. Thanks to Max sending a video message to you when he was supposed to send it to his dad, you—or rather we—are his only hope." He looked around at us all. "Jess can turn invisible, Heather can walk through walls, I can stop time, and Izzy is the best person I know at organizing things. All we have to do is find a way to put together our brains and our powers to rescue Max before Finch does something terrible to him or finds out about all of us and before Dr. Malone loses his job and his research."

I stared at Tom. "Um. Yeah, that's pretty much it," I said. When he put it like that, the odds didn't feel hugely in our favor. But then I looked at the three of them. We might not have an answer yet, but Tom was right. We had a bunch of superpowers between us, four brains, and forty-five minutes before our next class. We could do this.

"Look, I don't know how we're going to solve this," I said. "I just know that we have to and we can. We're a team now, and we stick together. Anything that hurts one of us hurts us all. So, as far as I'm concerned, we don't leave this room till we've come up with a way of rescuing Max. And we have to do it tonight. We're not leaving him in there a minute longer than we have to. So, are you in?"

Heather stared at me. Tom nodded. Izzy smiled. Then, as one, the three of them answered, "We're in!"

Ten minutes later, Heather was looking troubled. Well, we were all looking troubled. We had a fairly hefty problem to solve and only about half an hour left of our lunch break in which to do it. But she looked extra bothered.

"What's up?" I asked.

"Something's been confusing me about Max," Heather said. "I don't want to distract everyone from coming up with a rescue plan, but I don't understand—and it might help me think of something if I did."

"Go on," I told her.

"Well, if we have these powers because we were all born on the same day and delivered by your mom's friend, then how come Max has them? He wasn't born on the thirtieth of March, was he?"

"No," I said. "His birthday is in September."

"So how come he has a power?" Tom asked.

I didn't want to get into a long and complicated explanation, especially when I was hardly sure of the answer myself—and when planning a rescue was more important than getting to grips with why *any* of this was happening—but they deserved some kind of answer. I'd been thinking about the same question since my talk with Nancy earlier that morning, and I'd put a few of the pieces together.

"Max's dad was giving his mom the serum while she was pregnant with him," I said.

"Whoa!" Heather held a perfectly manicured hand up to her face. "He was experimenting on his own wife? That's gross!"

"No. He wasn't experimenting." I paused. "He was trying to save her life. That's how this whole thing started. Max's mom was dying. Dr. Malone was trying to find a cure."

"And?" Tom asked gently.

I shook my head.

Heather flushed. "I'm sorry. OK, now I want to help Max even more."

"I know what you mean," I agreed.

"But I still don't understand why the serum affected him—and us—and no one else," she insisted.

"Nancy told me how she thought it got into us so easily because a newborn baby's cells are multiplying so quickly," I began.

Tom's eyes widened as he realized where I was going. "And a baby that's still in the womb is growing even faster. So there's even *more* chance of it picking up the properties of the serum through its mother."

"Wow," Heather said. "That's, like . . ."

"Creepy?" Izzy suggested.

"I was going to say kind of miraculous," Heather said softly. She shot a look at Izzy from under her eyelashes. That shy smile again. The one I'd never seen before this week. "And maybe a bit creepy, too," she added.

Izzy smiled back.

"So," I said. "We've got three superpowers and four brains. Surely between us we can figure out how to get Max back!"

Izzy cleared her throat. "Um . . ." she said.

I looked at her. "What is it?"

"I just . . . I haven't got any powers," she said. "I don't really belong in the group."

"Of course you belong!" Tom exclaimed. "It doesn't matter if you haven't got a superpower."

"Are you sure?" Izzy asked. She turned to me— which was when I had a thought. A rather amazing thought—and possibly a slightly risky one, too. It had been simmering in the back of my mind for the last couple of days, but it was only as Izzy met my eyes that I fully acknowledged it as a real possibility. I glanced at my watch. We had time. And if it worked, it might even help us stand a better chance of rescuing Max.

I picked up my bag and rooted around inside. There! The bottle of serum that I hadn't managed to return to the lab.

Tom leaned in. "What's that?"

"It's the serum," I said.

"Whoa!" Heather said. "Really? Isn't it dangerous for anyone except us?"

I shook my head.

"Why haven't they tried it themselves, then?" asked Heather.

"They think it's dangerous for *adults.* They think there's a chance that it could have sped up Max's mom's death. It's all a bit complicated, but it's about the . . . What's it called? The front part of the brain."

"The frontal lobe?" Tom suggested.

"That's it. Once the frontal lobe is fully formed, the serum can be dangerous."

"But at our age, the brain is still in the process of forming," Tom added, "so that means it's not dangerous?"

"That's right. As far as we know." I looked at the bottle. There was hardly anything left inside it, but perhaps there would be just enough. I turned to Izzy. "It's up to you."

Izzy stared at the bottle. Then she held out her hand for it.

"Do you still have the crystal that Nancy gave you?" I asked.

Izzy blushed as if she'd been caught. "I . . . well, yes," she stammered. "I mean, I've always known it won't do anything, but I thought it couldn't do any harm to wear it anyway." She reached under her collar and pulled out a leather cord that was around her neck. Looped onto it, through its tiny hole, was the mini purple tower. The amethyst.

I held on to the bottle. "Izzy, are you sure?"

She nibbled on the end of her little finger. Then she nodded. "I'm positive," she said. "If it's not risky for you guys, it's not going to be risky for me. Nancy told us there were only a few bottles left, and they still haven't managed to re-create the original serum yet. This might be my only chance."

"Your only chance to do what, though?" Heather asked.

Izzy turned to her and smiled. Then she opened the bottle and drank the contents. Smiling, she closed her eyes. "Watch this," she said, "and you'll see."

I'm not sure which of us was the most surprised as Izzy slowly rose into the air. Tom and Heather stared open-jawed as she hovered about six inches off the floor and stayed there for five seconds before dropping back down with a bit of a stumble.

Izzy's face was a picture of utter astonishment and delight. "It worked! It worked!" she cried. "And I feel fine!" She threw her arms around me. "Thank you so much!" she exclaimed. "You're the best friend in the entire universe!"

As she pulled away from me, she gave us all

such a big grin you'd have thought—well, I guess you'd have thought she'd just discovered she could fly.

"Izzy, how on earth could you do it right away?" I asked.

Izzy blushed. She took her glasses off and wiped the lenses.

"You've been practicing, haven't you?" Tom teased as she put her glasses back on.

"Maybe just a little bit," Izzy admitted.

I laughed.

"I don't know how much help I can be yet," Izzy said. "But I'll work on it. We've got double history this afternoon. Jess, tell Mr. Robbins I'm sick and had to go home. I'll do nothing but practice all afternoon so I'll be ready to be part of Max's rescue."

"I'll join you," Tom said. "I've been given the afternoon off for Math Olympics practice, but this is more important."

"Great. Heather and I have already gotten used to our powers, so we should be OK." I checked my watch. "But only if we've got a plan before afternoon classes start. Otherwise, we *all* skip our classes and focus on this."

"OK," Izzy said, flipping open a notebook and

popping the lid of her pen. "Let's make a plan."

"Bottom line," I began. "We need to find out as much as we can about Finch—especially where he lives. Then somehow get to his house and get Max back."

Tom was already firing up his laptop. "I'll Google him. There must be something about him somewhere online."

Izzy leaned across to look over Tom's shoulder. "Good idea. Maybe his address will be there somewhere."

Tom frowned as he scanned through pages and links. "Nope," he said. "Nothing like that, as far as I can see. But, then, I didn't really think there would be. Who puts their home address on the Internet?"

"How are we going to find his house, then?" Heather asked.

"Wait. Maybe we don't need to." I played them Max's video again. When it finished, I looked around to see if anyone had had the same thought as me. Three blank faces stared back at me. "Finch is going to the lab at six," I prompted them.

"We can find him there!" Tom burst out. "Follow him home."

"What, all four of us?" Heather asked. "Without being seen?"

"Heather's right," Izzy said. "Jess could turn invisible, so she could get away with it, but what about the rest of us?"

Tom smiled slowly at us all. "Hang on," he said. "I've got an idea."

We all listened as he explained his idea. Then we spent the final fifteen minutes of our lunch break developing and refining it until we'd come up with something that might actually stand a chance of succeeding.

By the time the bell rang again, we'd more or less gotten it sorted out. We'd completely forgotten about eating any lunch, and the afternoon was going to be filled with growly stomachs and ditching classes and practicing newly discovered powers. But that was just fine—because we had a plan.

We were going to rescue Max and stop Finch. Tonight.

Chapter 20

Later that afternoon, Heather and I found ourselves in the unusual position of hanging out together over milk shakes. The milk shakes were fine. It was the hanging out together part that was unusual.

We'd all agreed to meet at the Corporation Street Café, around the corner from Dr. Malone's lab. Heather and I had come straight from school. I guessed Tom and Izzy were still practicing their new powers. As Heather and I had never spent three seconds alone in each other's company before, I prayed that the others would get here soon.

"You know. It's weird. I've always wanted to do this," Heather said as she stirred her milk shake with her straw.

I looked across at her. "Huh? You've always wanted to meet up with three people you barely know and discuss plans for breaking into some-one's house to rescue a boy you don't much like?"

Heather laughed softly. "No. Not that. Just, well . . . I've always kind of wished we could hang out."

I was glad I wasn't sipping my drink at that point or I might have choked to death on the spot. "You—you . . ." I spluttered. "But you're, like, Miss Super-Popular. You have half the girls in the grade trailing behind you and all the boys drooling over you."

"Exactly," Heather said. "Trailing and drool-ing. They're not exactly the best signs of friendship. *You* don't do either of those things. You always just seem to have fun. And be yourself."

"Can't really be anyone else," I said, trying to hide my surprise behind a joke.

Heather played with the straw. "You know what I mean," she said. "You don't have to wear and say and do all the right things all the time. You don't have to worry in case your image slips and you lose one of your followers. You don't have to try to be perfect all the time because that's what everyone expects from you. I like it. I guess . . . I like you. And I'm glad that we might be kind of, sort of, maybe starting to be friends."

She stared into her milk shake. I could see the tops of her cheeks had flushed.

"Hey," I said without stopping to think. "We're *definitely* kind of, sort of, starting to be friends."

Heather looked up and smiled. I felt *my* cheeks heat up a bit. Luckily, at that moment, the door opened. Tom and Izzy burst in, and I didn't have time to dwell on why I was so pleased that Heather seemed to like me.

"All right, let's go over it one last time," Izzy said as she slurped her chocolate milk shake. We'd all told our parents we were studying at each other's houses and had been discussing the finer details of our plan for the last half hour.

Tom took a bite out of his cookie. "Jess goes invisible and waits at the end of the road," he said as if he were reciting something he'd memorized for a test. "When Jess sees Finch on his way to the lab, she texts me. I stop time, come out of hiding, and search Finch for anything with his address on it."

"How do you know you'll be able to stop time for long enough to search him?" Heather asked.

"I've done virtually nothing but practice since yesterday. I managed about five minutes earlier this afternoon with Izzy. That should easily be long enough to frisk a few pockets."

"Just be as quick as you can, won't you?" Izzy said.

Tom smiled. "'Course."

"And you're double-sure you can touch him while you've stopped time and he won't know about it?" I asked, checking.

Tom nodded. "Yup. Tested that, too. I'm double-*triple* sure. It'll all be fine, honest."

"OK, so as soon as Tom and Jess get back here, we flag down a cab and get to Finch's place as quick as we can," Heather continued.

"And we cross every finger and toe we've got that that's where Max is being held," I put in. He *had* to be there. The idea that he could be somewhere else and we'd have no chance of finding him was unthinkable.

"Yep," Tom agreed. "Then I ring the bell, sweet and innocent, to check that there's no one else there," he went on. "If anyone answers, I ask them if they'd like to donate to the Boy Scouts and we abort the plan and regroup."

"If no one answers the door, Tom gives me a thumbs-up," Heather put in. "Then I go through one of the walls, find the nearest door, and let the rest of you in."

"Preferably a door around the back, so we'll be out of sight," I reminded her.

"Then we creep through the house as quietly as we can—just in case there *is* anyone there and they ignored the door," Izzy added. "We search the house for Max and get him out."

"And while we're at it, we look for anything that Finch might have stolen from the lab and confiscate it," I finished.

Foolproof.

"How long do you think Finch will wait outside the lab before he realizes the doctor's not coming?" Heather asked.

I shrugged. "He seems like a man who knows what he wants and is determined to get it. Let's hope that means he'll wait."

Tom glanced at his watch. "It's quarter to six. You ready?"

I nodded. "Let's get into our starting positions."

I popped into the bathroom while the others headed outside. Once I'd turned myself invisible, I joined them. "OK, let's go."

"Good luck," Izzy whispered. I grimaced nervously in reply. Not that any of them saw me.

I'd been waiting at the end of Albany Road for just over five minutes when I saw him round the corner. Oscar Finch was difficult to miss. A very tall man in an immaculate suit, walking purposefully toward the lab—and toward me.

My heart started to do a quickstep. It threw in a few pirouettes when I noticed what Finch had with him—a large German shepherd, pulling on its leash and slobbering as it showed its teeth. Even if Finch didn't know I was here, his dog might. I grabbed my phone and, with shaking fingers, texted Tom as quickly as I could.

Finch kept walking. He was about twenty paces away from me. *Tom, hurry, please!*

A moment later, I saw Tom emerge from the bushes, and then—before I even knew what was happening or what *had* happened—Finch had walked past me and Tom was by my side. "Jess, are you there?" he whispered furiously. "It's done. Let's get out of here."

"I'm here!" I whispered back. Then I held my breath and followed him as fast as I could. Had

Tom done his part already? Had he stopped time? Did we have Finch's address? Were we really going to go and save Max?

My head swam with questions as we hurried to join the others.

Five minutes later, we were in a taxi, speeding toward Finch's house: Charlesworthy Mansion on Briary Road. The rich end of town, unsurprisingly.

"Where did you find his address, Tom?" Heather asked.

"Searched his jacket pockets. It was on his driver's license."

"Amazing," Izzy breathed, looking out the window as we left the apartment buildings behind and entered wider, leafy streets with huge houses.

A couple of minutes later, we turned onto Briary Road. Charlesworthy Mansion was halfway down.

We paid the taxi driver and took in our surroundings while we watched him drive away. Whatever Finch did for a living, it was obvious that he made tons of money doing it. Charlesworthy Mansion was the biggest house I'd ever seen.

We walked for what felt like half a mile up a tree-lined drive. It led to a house that looked a bit like one of those stately homes your grandparents visit on Sunday afternoons.

Heather, Izzy, and I kept out of sight while Tom went to the door. He pressed the bell and waited. Nothing. He pressed again. Still nothing. The coast was clear. He turned in our direction and gave a thumbs-up.

Heather let out a heavy breath. "All right. My turn," she said.

I touched her arm. "You'll be fine," I told her.

She gave me a nervous smile. "See you on the other side. Go to the back and—don't forget—keep quiet once we get in the house; there might still be someone inside."

With that, she followed a path to the side of the building, glanced around—and then walked through the side wall into Finch's house.

I stared after her for a moment. I mean, I'd had time to get used to my own powers, but it was still a bit weird watching someone else use theirs.

"Come on." Tom shook me out of my thoughts. I joined him and Izzy, and we ran around to the back of the house. We were in luck. Finch had a back door that was completely hidden from view. A second later, there was a rustling sound on the other side. I prayed that it wasn't an unexpected houseguest.

It wasn't. Heather opened the door, and we hurried into the house.

We stood in the hallway and looked around. It was like the foyer of a fancy hotel.

"Now what?" Heather asked in a whisper. "Where do we start?"

We looked blankly at one another. I mean, it was all very well having a plan, but now that we were actually inside Finch's house, it didn't feel quite so straightforward.

I took charge. "We try every door," I whispered back. "Tom and Izzy, you take the first floor. Heather and I will take the second floor. If anyone sees anything, come and get the others, and we'll all deal with it together. OK?"

The others nodded.

Izzy checked her watch. "It's quarter past six already. We still don't know how long Finch will wait, but I figure we've got half an hour, tops."

Heather was already halfway up the stairs. "Come on," she said. "Let's get looking."

The first couple of doors we tried looked like guest bedrooms—perfectly made beds, polished surfaces, and nothing that seemed of any interest to us at all.

We moved on to a door at the far end of the

corridor. Heather reached for the door handle, and we peeked inside. Still no Max. It looked like Finch's office. A huge desk ran the length of one wall, with a photocopier at the end; filing cabinets and cupboards lined the other.

"This stuff looks important," Heather said. "Have we got time to check it out?"

"Not really," I said. Then I glanced at the desk. It was overflowing with piles of papers covered in charts and graphs and lists. What if he'd stolen them from the lab? What was the point in rescuing Max if Finch had enough information to figure out what was going on and pose a threat to us forever?

"OK, let's take just one minute," I said. "Grab everything that looks relevant and then move on."

I picked up a handful of papers. I was right! This was definitely research from the lab! There were more papers stacked up across his desk. I took those, too. Finch had stolen all of Dr. Malone's notes! My blood started to bubble inside me. How dare he!

I was snatching up paperwork, scrunching and folding it and shoving it in my school bag, when Heather stopped me. "Jess," she said.

I looked up.

Heather was holding an identical bottle to the one I'd given to Izzy. The serum!

"It was under some papers," she said.

I paused for a millisecond. "Take it," I said firmly. "This man is dangerous. He already got the research notes *and* the serum. It won't take long for him to join the dots and find out about all of us. You saw the video. You heard his threats to Max. I heard him on the phone in the lab. He'll want to experiment on us. He will sell anything and everything to whoever offers him the most money. This man is evil and dangerous, and we *have* to stop him."

Heather nodded. "OK," she agreed, and put the bottle in her pocket.

"All right, come on. Let's get out of here," I said.

As we closed the study door behind us, Tom and Izzy were rounding the top of the stairs.

"Anything?" Izzy asked.

We told her what we'd found.

"How about you?" Heather said.

"Nothing downstairs," Tom replied. He nodded to another staircase. "You been up there yet?"

I shook my head and started toward the stairs. "Let's go."

I was halfway up the staircase when Izzy grabbed me. "Jess!" She pointed out the landing window. It looked out over the long driveway. The driveway along which a large German shepherd and a very tall man were marching none too happily toward the house.

I froze.

"What do we do?" Izzy whispered.

Tom bit his thumbnail. "We need to go. He'll be here any minute."

"What about Max?" I insisted.

"He could be anywhere," Heather said. "We'll never find him before Finch gets home."

"Heather's right," Tom said. "If we're still in Finch's house when he gets back, it's game over. He sees us and we're toast."

That was it! Of course! We couldn't run the risk of him *seeing* us. That meant *we* couldn't be here. But it didn't mean *I* couldn't be here.

"You go," I said. "I'll stay."

Izzy shook her head. "We're not leaving you. We're in this together. We're a team."

"I'll make myself invisible. I'll be silent." I shoved them toward the stairs and switched my phone onto silent. "Go, all of you. Out the back door. I'll lock it behind you. He'll never know you were here. Hide somewhere nearby and text me so I know where to find you. I'm not leaving here without Max."

Heather looked worried. "You're sure?"

"It's the only option. Go on. Go. Quickly."

"We'll be hiding near the end of the driveway," Izzy said. "We won't leave till you're both out of here and all right."

A minute later, the three of them had gone and the house was quiet. I turned myself invisible and breathed a sigh of relief. OK, I was safe.

For now.

❋

I was on the top landing when I heard the front door open. I'd had a quick look in two of the rooms and had another four to go.

I opened another door. Nothing. Where *was* Max?

I tiptoed out of the room and back into the corridor. "Max!" I said under my breath, cursing myself for not having simply shouted out his name the minute we'd entered the house. I certainly couldn't do it now.

Three more doors on this floor. All closed. I

tiptoed toward the first one and turned the handle. The door wouldn't open.

"Oscar?" A voice called from inside. Max! I'd found him!

"It's me!" I whispered.

"Jess?"

I leaned close to the door. *"Shhhh.* I've come to rescue you. The door's locked."

"There's a ledge at the end of the hallway," Max said. "It's where he keeps his spare keys."

"How do you know?"

"I heard him get it once. He has a key ring there for emergencies. He doesn't usually use it, but once he must have forgotten his key. Hopefully he won't miss it if it's gone."

My heart racing like a runaway train, I ran to the end of the hallway as silently as I could. Then I stood on my tiptoes, reached up, and ran my hand along a dusty shelf. My fingers hit on something metal. Got it!

I ran back to Max's door and fumbled with the keys as quickly and quietly as I could. There were about ten of them on the ring, and I couldn't find the right one. I was trying the fourth when something else suddenly became a bit more pressing.

The dog.

It started barking from the downstairs hallway. "Jess, quick!" Max yelped from inside the room. My hands were shaking so much I could barely hold the keys, let alone use them. Finally, I put another one in the lock, and miraculously, I'd gotten the right one this time.

I pushed the door open and crept inside.

"Lock the door again or he'll be suspicious!" Max said right away.

I did. Then I turned to look at him. He seemed thinner—which was ridiculous because I'd only seen him yesterday. But he definitely looked different. He'd lost his cocky swagger. His hair was even more of a mess than usual. His eyes were dark.

He was sitting on a bed in a corner of the room, peering vaguely in my direction. "I'm guessing you are actually there," he said.

I'd forgotten I was invisible. "Oh, yes. Sorry, I'll—"

"No!" Max stopped me. "Stay invisible. In case he comes in."

The dog must have come up the first set of stairs, as the barking and whining had gotten louder.

"Ivor, stop it. Behave!" Finch's voice called from downstairs.

I stood, frozen like a statue, and waited to see what was going to happen next.

"There's nothing there. What's the matter?" Finch snapped.

I knew what was the matter. Ivor could tell there'd been intruders. He could probably still smell me.

A second later, Ivor had clearly had enough of being told there was nothing there. I heard him bound up the second set of stairs and along the hallway, growling. He stopped outside the door and barked furiously.

"Ivor, come downstairs this minute!" Finch was shouting. "What on *earth* is wrong with you?"

I looked at Max. His face was as white as mine probably would have been—if I hadn't been invisible.

"What do we do?" I whispered.

Max shook his head. "I don't know. Maybe he'll calm down."

The barking grew louder and snarlier.

"You think?"

Max swallowed.

Finch shouted up the stairs. "Do I have to come and get you?"

NO! No, please don't!

It seemed he answered his own question, though, as a moment later I heard footsteps on the stairs. This was it, then. I had about thirty seconds before becoming dog food.

"Just stay invisible, and Finch won't know you're here," Max said. "And try not to panic. Dogs can smell fear."

Oh. Lovely. Thanks for the great advice, Max.

I heard Finch's voice grumbling, a key turning—and then the door opened.

"Now, what's all the fuss about?" Finch asked, looking around the room as he held on to Ivor by the collar. "It's *Max*," he said, sugar sweet. "He's our *guest*. You *know* Max. He's nothing to get upset about."

I tried to do what Max had said and stay calm, even though I felt as if my heart were about to bounce right out of the top of my head like a jack-in-the-box.

It wasn't easy. See, Ivor knew better than Finch. He was still growling, his teeth bared and white saliva dripping from the edge of his mouth. Ivor wasn't happy at all.

His lips curled as he narrowed his eyes.

The eyes that didn't seem to care that I was invisible, because they were looking directly at me.

Chapter 21

I had to get out of there. Mainly because if I didn't, I was about to get mauled to death by an angry dog. Also, Finch was no idiot. If he knew anything about the superpowers, it wouldn't take him long to figure out that someone invisible might be in the room.

Besides, I was finding it harder and harder to keep my mind calm and blank. A couple of my fingernails had already started to show, so I did the only thing I could.

I held my breath and edged as carefully and quietly as possible out of the room.

Ivor's eyes followed me. Luckily, Finch was holding on to his collar so he stayed where he was. For now.

I tiptoed past Finch, terrified that he'd move and bump into me. He didn't. I made it out onto the landing. I took a breath and tried to calm down enough to think about my next step.

"See. That's better, isn't it?" Finch was saying to the dog. "Now, then. Let me deal with my next problem." He turned his eyes to Max. "You."

"M-me?" Max said in a voice I'd never heard him use before. He sounded much less like the tough guy he pretended to be and more like the terrified boy I imagined he actually was right now.

"*Someone's* been giving me the runaround," Finch replied. "I waited at the lab for half an hour. No Dr. Malone. Why's that, huh?" His voice was smooth like honey, but with a thin strand of cold steel running through it. "I don't like being jerked around," he said slowly. "People who wrong me do not go unpunished. Do you understand?"

"Y-yes," Max replied. "I didn't . . . I haven't . . . I—"

"Enough!" Finch cut him off. "I'll think about what to do with you later. Right now, I've got work to do."

Work? In his office? No! I couldn't let him go in there! He'd see that everything was gone. What was I going to do?

"Come on, Ivor," he said to the dog. "Dinnertime first." Finch turned back to Max as he paused in the doorway. "I don't want to hear a peep out of you," he said. Then he closed the door and locked it behind him.

I had to hide, before Ivor sensed me out here. I looked both ways and opened the first door I could see—which led into a closet filled with boxes, books, and about twenty pairs of boots. I slipped inside, pulled the door closed, and waited in the darkness.

I heard Finch lock Max's door, and to my relief, he and the dog headed down the stairs. Luckily for me, the word "dinner" clearly had more appeal than an invisible intruder who now seemed to have left—aka me.

A moment later, the hallway was silent and my body remembered how to breathe.

I opened the closet door and peered out. The coast was clear. Silently, I crept back to Max's room. "Max," I whispered through the door. "Are you OK?"

I heard a sound from inside. I couldn't be sure, but I think he might have been crying. "I'm fine," he said, "but I have to get out of here. Jess, you've got to think of something."

What could I do? I was here on my own, the others had gone, and Finch was not in a good mood. Surely we were out of options.

"Max, maybe I need to call the police," I said.

"No! It's too risky. We can't let them know about the lab. My dad could lose his job. He might even go to prison. And we're inside Finch's house! He'll find some way to twist it. You don't know what he's like. He'll probably say we broke in and have us arrested."

Max was right. And, in my case at least, Finch would be telling the truth. I *had* broken into his house.

"Please, Jess, think of something else."

"I'm trying," I whispered. I pretended I hadn't noticed the gulping and sobbing noises in between Max's words.

Come on, Jessica. Think. Think. I probably had about five minutes. If only Izzy were still here. She'd know what to do.

Wait. Izzy *was* still here. OK, she was outside hiding, but she'd said they'd wait. Maybe she could do something. Knock on the door. Say she was lost. Come up with a way to get us out of here. I knew she'd think of something.

I pulled out my phone and typed as fast as I

could. "Found Max. Locked in back room on top floor. Help! Need to get out. Do something!" I sent the text to Izzy. Then I got Finch's spare keys out of my pocket, silently turned the key in the lock, and let myself back into Max's room.

Max glanced up and quickly dragged a sleeve across his face as I came in. "I've got a cold," he said quickly. "Hay fever."

I locked the door behind me and made myself visible. It was exhausting trying to remain invisible, and at least for a few minutes, it didn't matter. "It's fine," I said, and Max nodded miserably.

"What are we going to do?" he asked.

"I'm not sure. If worst comes to worst, we'll just have to make a run for it. Sneak out of the house somehow."

"We can't! He'll catch us. Ivor will kill us!"

"Yeah, there is that," I admitted. "Look, I've texted Izzy. She'll think of something," I went on, trying to sound more confident than I felt. I glanced out the window. "Does this open?" I asked.

"Yeah." Max came over and pushed the window open. "Not that there's much point," he said. "We're three floors up and there are no pipes or ledges to climb out onto. I've looked out of here at least a hundred times trying to find a means of escape, but I thought if I didn't kill myself, at the very least I'd break every bone in my body." He closed the window again.

"Finch knew what he was doing when he chose this room."

"Yup."

I looked at my phone. No reply from Izzy. Had she received my text? Was she thinking of a way to get us out? Why wasn't she knocking on the front door to distract Finch? Why wasn't she doing *something*? We were running out of time. As soon as Finch had fed the dog, he was going to his office—and then he'd see that it had been ransacked.

Where *was* she? What if Finch had caught them? What if Izzy—?

My thoughts were interrupted by a tapping sound. "Max, stop drumming your fingers on the desk," I said. "I'm trying to think."

"I'm not drumming my fingers," Max said woodenly. Then he gasped. "Jess!"

I turned to look at him. "What?"

He was pointing at the window. "Isn't that Izzy?"

I swung around to face the window. It *was* Izzy! She was here! Outside the window. Hovering in the air three floors up and gesturing wildly at the glass!

Did she want to come in? I couldn't let her. Finch would be back soon. I couldn't let him catch all three of us!

"OPEN IT!" Izzy mouthed, jabbing her hand even more frantically at the window.

Just then, a familiar sound started up on the other side of the door. The sound of a barking German shepherd coming up the stairs. He'd obviously finished his dinner and decided it was time for dessert—aka me.

Finch's voice wasn't far behind him. "Ivor!" he boomed. "If I have to come up there and drag you down, there's going to be trouble."

He had that right. A whole lot of trouble. For me and Max, though—not for the dog. Ivor would be a hero.

We didn't waste any more time. Max opened the window, and I ran over to join him.

"Get on my back!" Izzy told Max.

"Get on . . ."

"My back. Yes. Hurry."

Max looked at me and I suddenly realized why

he was in so much shock. The last he knew, Izzy didn't have any superpower, and now she was flying around in the sky and ordering him to join her. I was almost as shocked myself. I'd only seen her rise a tiny bit off the floor. I guess this is what happens when you spend all afternoon practicing something that's been a lifelong ambition.

"We'll explain later," I said to Max. "Go."

Without another word, Max grabbed his bag and clambered out of the window and onto Izzy's back.

"Hold tight," she said. Over her shoulder, she added, "I'll be back for you in a couple of minutes."

As they flew off, Max clutching onto Izzy, Izzy looking as if she'd been flying all her life, I prayed that a couple of minutes would be soon enough.

Thirty seconds. Izzy and Max flew over the lawn.

A minute. They were out of sight.

A minute and a half. Ivor was right outside the door. And so was Finch. "All right," he said from the other side of a tiny bit of wood. "What on *earth* is going on?"

I used every bit of mental energy I had to calm enough of my mind so I could turn invisible again. Not that it would do much good. As soon as that door was open, the dog would be on me. Plus, it would take Finch about a squillionth of a second to register that Max was gone.

A minute and three quarters. The key was turning in the lock.

Izzy! Please hurry!

I probably had ten seconds before Finch and Ivor were in the room and I was dessert. I was about to give up. Tears burned my eyes. I wished I could have said good-bye to Mom and Dad. Wished I could have done better at school. Wished I—

"Jess!"

Izzy! She was back!

Still invisible, I clambered out of the window and onto Izzy's back so fast that I almost jumped right over her. I grabbed onto her sweater to stop myself from falling.

"Ouch!" Izzy yelped.

"Sorry! I was in a hurry!"

I straightened myself out and held on firmly.

"Ready?" Izzy asked.

"Ready."

As we flew away from the house and across the lawn, I glimpsed the room I'd left behind— the door opening, a slathering German shepherd bounding through, Finch close behind, his shocked face.

"NOOOOOO!" he screamed. He probably screamed lots of other things, too, but we didn't hear the rest of it. We were too busy flying to the bushes at the edge of his yard, landing softly to join the others, and getting the heck away from there as fast as we could.

"I can't believe we did it!" Izzy said, smiling broadly as the five of us slurped our drinks back at the Corporation Street Café and listened as Max told us about his time with Finch.

"How did he get away with it?" asked Tom. "How did he get you there in the first place?"

Max frowned. "I was an idiot. He drove past while I was waiting for the bus to school and he offered me a lift. I decided it would be a good opportunity to confront him about being at the lab, so I got in the car. He was super smooth. Said he could explain everything, but we'd have to take a detour. I wasn't exactly upset about not getting to school on time, so I agreed."

"Couldn't you read his mind while you were in the car?" Heather asked.

Max grimaced. "The leather cord for my hematite skull snapped this morning when I was getting dressed. I'd been planning to fix it when I got to school, so the hematite was in my bag."

"So you didn't have it next to your skin," I said.

"And you couldn't exactly start fumbling around in your bag for it when the last thing you wanted to do was make him suspicious," Tom added.

"Exactly," agreed Max. "In other words, I pretty much sat back and did nothing while he drove me to his house and locked me in a room."

"Don't blame yourself," Heather said gently. "I'd probably have fallen for it, too. He seems like a persuasive kind of guy."

"Yeah. That's the weird thing. He seemed so nice and so believable—even when I was fairly certain he was up to something shady. I never even questioned how he'd found us in the first place."

"I bet he kept an eye on your dad for years," Izzy suggested.

"And then started keeping watch when he saw that Dr. Malone had opened a new lab," Heather added.

"Probably." Max thought for a moment. "He was never horrible to me, you know," he went on. "He didn't keep me tied up or anything, and he fed me decent food. He was really friendly the whole time. It made him even creepier, in a way. To my face, he was nice—but I was right there when he made all those threats on the video, as you saw."

"He didn't need to be nasty to your face," I said. "He just needed to keep you there long enough to get to your dad."

"And he failed," Heather added.

"Yeah. He failed to get to my dad—and we succeeded in doing all this without Dad even knowing a thing about it!"

"We really did it," Tom mused. "We stopped the bad guy. A bunch of kids against one super-evil brain. Not bad, really."

Izzy took her glasses off and cleaned them with a napkin. "But did we, though?" she asked. "I mean—have we *definitely* stopped him?"

"Totally!" Tom replied. "We got his stuff, and Nancy told Jess they've changed the keycode at the lab. He's not going to get back in there."

"And there's no way *anyone's* going to give him the number again," Max added.

"He wouldn't dare do anything now, anyway," Heather put in. "He won't come within a hundred miles of Max, if he knows what's good for him. As far as he's concerned, Max could quite easily march up to the nearest police station and have him charged with kidnapping a minor."

"Heather's right," I said, holding up my phone. "We still have the video as evidence, so he *better* not bother *any* of us again!"

Max grinned. "Thanks to you guys."

"And thanks to the fact that Finch never checked who you'd sent the video to," Tom said.

"It's lucky he believed my explanation," Max added.

"That was a stroke of genius," I agreed. "Managing to convince Finch that 'J' was for James, your dad."

"Yeah. Thank goodness your name starts with the same letter as Dad's!" Max said. "If I hadn't fooled Finch about that, I'd probably still be there now."

I looked at Max. I realized I'd underestimated him. I guessed most people probably did.

"Thanks," he said. Then he smiled at me. A real smile. No sarcasm, no jokes, no teasing to cover anything up. "Really," he said. "I mean it. Thank you. For everything."

I smiled back. Then I started feeling a bit silly, so I took a sip of my hot chocolate.

When I looked up again, I spotted someone

hurrying by the window — someone who happened to glance in at the same moment. Nancy! She must have been on her way to the lab.

She stopped walking as she noticed me. Then she turned and came into the café.

"Hi, Nancy," I said, giving her my best *I'm-just-having-a-drink-with-my-school-friends-not-discussing-anything-to-do-with-superpowers-or-evil-thieving-kidnappers-who-you-happen-to-know-at-all* smile.

"Hey, Jess. Hi, Izzy," she said. She glanced around at the others. Then she noticed Max. "Hi, Max . . . I didn't know you two knew each other." She raised her eyebrows in a *care-to-explain-at-all?* kind of way.

She knew! We'd been busted! We hadn't managed to keep this secret for five minutes. Nancy would make us own up and tell everyone. What could I say?

Before I'd thought of anything, Heather burst out, "Science project!"

Nancy turned to Heather. So did the rest of us.

Heather gave Nancy her best smile. "We all got put into groups for a project we're doing this semester," she said, slick as anything. Well, who would have guessed that Heather class-president

Berry would turn out to be such a good liar?

"And I got lumped in with this lot," Max added with a grimace and a *well-what-can-you-do?* kind of shrug.

Nancy nodded slowly. Then she smiled. "Well, good for you," she said. "Enjoy your project."

She believed us. At least, she was happy to go along with the pretense that she did. Either way, I was fairly sure of two things: one, Nancy wasn't going to give us away, and two, we now had the perfect excuse to keep on meeting up without any of our parents getting suspicious about the new group of friends we'd suddenly made.

As Nancy left us to it, the five of us let out a collective breath.

"We did it," Heather said, grinning broadly.

"We did, didn't we?" Max agreed.

"Incredible," added Tom, shaking his head in proud disbelief.

Izzy turned to me. "Think we've earned the right to call ourselves superheroes yet?" she asked with a smile. "Even just slightly?"

I made a face as I pretended to think about it. "Nah, we're not slightly superheroes at all," I said. Izzy's face dropped, till I added, "We are *totally* superheroes!"

"Right!" Max agreed. He held out his cup, and we each held up our drinks in a toast.

As we clinked them together, Max announced, "To the five of us. Totally superheroes."

"Totally superheroes," we all repeated.

And I'm pretty sure it wasn't just the hot chocolate that made me feel warm inside.

On Friday morning, I was up, dressed, and at school half an hour early.

It was weird. In one way, nothing had changed. The day was still going to start with English and end with double geography. It was still going to include being reprimanded by teachers multiple times for talking or not listening or not knowing the answer to something. It would still involve being given homework I'd rather scratch my eyes out than do.

To a casual observer, it was the same as any other day. But, on the inside, everything had changed.

From now on, Heather wouldn't put up with being worshipped and followed around by adoring fans. She had realized that *real* friends were people who liked you for who you were, instead of who you felt you had to pretend to be.

Tom would hold his head a bit higher and not care about the people who called him a geek, now that he had something that made him, in his words, "approximately a million to the power of a million" times cooler than them.

Max would spend time talking and laughing instead of grunting and scowling with his soccer friends, now that he'd discovered that he had people who cared about him.

Izzy would work just as hard in her classes, but she wouldn't worry so much about her grades having to be perfect. She'd be too busy grinning at the thought of all the things she could do, now that her biggest fantasy had come true.

And me? Well, yeah, I'd probably still get into trouble at school. I'd still be late for French; I'd still get scolded for passing notes in English or not listening in geography.

But none of it would matter. Because I still had my two best friends, and now we were closer than ever, and I also had a new friend to save me a seat in French and another who knew what I was thinking without my having to say anything. I had four people who would be at my side in a second if I needed them. A group of true friends to hatch plans with, to laugh and joke with, to share secrets with. To be myself with.

Those were the things that had changed for me. The things that mattered.

The things you couldn't see.

Dive in and read the
New York Times *best-selling series!*

www.candlewick.com